D1569356

The Gathering Dark

PAGE STREET
PUBLISHING CO.

Copyright © 2022 Erica Waters, Chloe Gong, Tori Bovalino, Hannah Whitten,
Allison Saft, Olivia Chadha, Courtney Gould, Aden Polydoros, Alex Brown,
Shakira Toussaint

First published in 2022 by
Page Street Publishing Co.
27 Congress Street, Suite 1511
Salem, MA 01970
www.pagestreetpublishing.com

Distributed by Macmillan, sales in Canada by The Canadian Manda Group.

26   25   24   23   22   2   3   4   5

ISBN-13: 978-1-64567-622-5
ISBN-10: 1-64567-622-6

Library of Congress Control Number: 2021953212

Cover and book design by Rosie Stewart for Page Street Publishing Co.
Cover illustration © Evangeline Gallagher

Printed and bound in the United States

Page Street Publishing protects our planet by donating to nonprofits like
The Trustees, which focuses on local land conservation.

An Anthology of Folk Horror

The Gathering Dark

Edited by Tori Bovalino

PAGE STREET
PUBLISHING CO.

Content Warning:
implied sexual abuse and trauma, body horror,
gore, violence, death of a child/teenager, mentions
of drug/substance abuse, terminal illness

Table of Contents

Stay

by Erica Waters

GRANNY THINKS THERE ARE WORMS LIVING BENEATH HER SKIN. It started when the doctor changed up her medications and she started complaining she was itchy. I bought her lotions and ointments and prescription-strength creams, but nothing helped.

Now she scratches all day long, until her arms are covered in red, bleeding sores. She swears the sores are from the worms tunneling through. I trimmed her nails down to the quick, so she found a pair of tweezers. For hours at a time, she'll sit staring at her skin under the lamplight, tweezers at the ready. Her dearest desire is to catch one and prove to me that she's not a senile old lady.

She glances up when I come into the living room, then goes right back to staring at her arm. "They take cover when they hear other people," she mutters. "They're always listening."

"Ask them if they know where I put my boots," I mutter back. Granny hears and snaps her head in my direction, suddenly as ferocious as the fat old Chihuahua who used to sit beside her all day. She made me give him away for fear she might transfer the worms to him.

"Sorry, Granny, but I'm late for work," I say.

"Your boots are under the recliner," she says in a sour voice. "You wouldn't lose them if you'd put them in your bedroom where they belong."

"Yes, ma'am," I say, relieved to see some of my old granny peeking through. She hasn't surrendered completely to the delusion of the worms. I dig my work boots out from beneath the chair where Papa used to sit every evening, watching reruns of *Bonanza*.

"Melissa, I think I see one!" Granny yells.

"I gotta go to work, Granny," I say, trying not to sigh.

"Just come look, you little shit," she says excitedly.

"Fine." I climb up off the floor and stand over her.

"You're blocking the light—move over there," she chides.

Her show of crankiness seems like a good sign, so I do as she asks and peer down at her arm. She points with the tweezers at her wrist, just below a blue-green vein. "There, do you see it? Do you see it moving under the skin? Lean down closer."

I lower my face closer to her arm, close enough that I can feel her breath on my hair. And then I do see something: the barest tremor of her wrinkled flesh, like a ripple on the surface of a pond. I swear and slap a hand over my mouth as I stumble away from her.

Granny cackles, gleeful in her triumph. "I told you! You said I was getting dementia, but I told you! I was right." Then her voice breaks off into a sob. "All these weeks I've told you, and I've told you, and you wouldn't listen. There are worms in my skin. There are worms!" Granny weeps, her soft shoulders trembling, tears flowing down her face and onto her housedress.

I don't know what to say, what to think. There was something there, something moving beneath her skin. But maybe I'm just tired. Maybe I've listened to her for so long, I'm becoming deluded too. Maybe it was just her pulse beating. I don't know what to believe. But my own skin crawls sympathetically.

I smooth down my grandmother's hair. "I'll take you back to the doctor on Monday," I promise. "I'll tell him what I saw."

Granny wipes her eyes. "Thank you, baby. Now get on. You're gon' be late for work, and then they're gonna fire your lazy, hard-headed behind," she says.

I pull on my boots and grab my bag on my way out the door. I back my truck out of the yard with its knee-high grass and onto the worn drive beneath the arching branches of the oak trees. It's a gloomy day, rain already drizzling. Under the hanging Spanish moss, the morning feels shadowy, shifting, slightly unreal. I drive slowly past the horse pasture, where my cousin's dappled Appaloosa stands at the fence looking sullen.

"Not my problem, not my problem, not my problem," I chant to myself. If Daniel can't get up early enough to feed his horse, that's not my problem. That horse is mean as the devil anyway.

"Damn it." I stop the truck and dig an apple out of my lunch and toss it into the pasture. "Not that you deserve it," I say as Mountain picks it up and bites into the fruit, one eye still on me. He's as watchful and bad-tempered as Granny.

When I near the gravel turn into the family cemetery, I bite my lip. It's raining and I'm already late for work. But I haven't tended the graves in a long while. The dead are starting to get restless. I can feel them, just under my skin, like one of Granny's phantom worms. I shudder. But when I look at the time on the old radio clock, I decide the dead are gonna have to wait.

I'll do it this afternoon, I promise them.

I'll go to the cemetery after work. I'll take Granny to the doctor on Monday. I'll go wake Daniel up from his drug haze and yell at him about his horse sometime in between. All the things waiting for me to deal with them, waiting sullen and restless and resentful, are just going to have to keep on waiting.

I drive past the cemetery with its white wooden fence, lichen-spotted, graying all over, dandelions pushing through the slats. The oaks and pines rise up around it in a semicircle like watchful gods. I don't look at the gravestones, which I know are covered in moss and mold and tree sap, their little whiskey bottles dirty, their pennies green with oxidation, their plastic flowers rotting. It's been too long since I've visited, too long since I've cleaned. Granny used to take care of it before the arthritis in her feet and knees got too bad. Now it's my job, and I'm failing.

I'm only one person, one girl, seventeen and still in high school. I ought to be doing my homework and falling in love. I ought to be dreaming of college and life after this place, but I can barely get past the mailbox at the end of our drive.

How much can you give to a place before it swallows you whole?

I drive the ten miles of flat, relentless highway, all green fields and skinny pines, cows in their pastures, trailers on their plots of land. And half a dozen family cemeteries just like mine, each one as potent as a preacher in his pulpit, wagging his finger at me.

In Lagerty, we bury our own dead and tend our own graves. We've done it so long, most people probably don't even know why anymore. But you learn grave lore right alongside the Ten Commandments and the Lord's Prayer. Tending your dead is as sacred as baptism.

This afternoon, I promise mine. *You'll have to keep till then.*

The second I see the welcome sign for the next town, I gun my engine, as if the border between here and there can defy limestone and soil and roots, can defy my restless dead and a hungry horse and an old woman with cracked and broken skin.

When I drive past the sign, I feel a pain in my forearm, like strong fingers pressing into my skin, trying to yank me back home. I squeeze the steering wheel harder and continue on, ignoring the sensation.

Just a tired mind imagining things, same as Granny.

When I pull into the gravel parking lot of the garden store, I breathe a sigh of relief. I've got eight whole hours away from home, eight whole hours of work. And tomorrow I'll have eight more.

The big iron gate is already rolled up, leaving the storefront open for customers. When I walk in, I'm hit with the scents of potting soil and fertilizers, chemical and caustic, the scent of false power. This smell tells customers they can control the natural world—that they can kill the weeds and keep the rot at bay, that aphids won't destroy their prize roses and slugs won't decimate their lettuces. That they can wield power over their lawns and gardens, over all the agents of decay. This smell is a lie.

But it's a lie I love, a reprieve. Sixteen hours of reprieve.

"Hey, Melissa," my boss, Lula, calls, not caring that I'm fifteen minutes late for my shift. She's a chubby middle-aged woman with permanently red cheeks and dirt-ringed fingernails. "Can you go help Shelly unload the truck?"

"Shelly's here?" I ask, stopping in my tracks. Lula winks at me and nods toward the back. I guess my crush on her daughter has not gone unnoticed.

Shelly is yanking potted dogwood saplings out of the back of the truck with alarming speed, her midriff tank showing off her biceps and abs and making me swoon a little where I stand.

Thoughts of home and Granny and the cemetery fade away as I watch her work.

She catches sight of me. "You gonna help me or what?" she asks with a laugh, and I feel my cheeks burn as red as Lula's. I wish I could think of something witty to say, but I just scramble forward and start pulling down trees too.

Shelly is eighteen and a freshman at UF. She comes in sometimes on the weekends to help out her mom. She never says much when she's here.

We work in silence for a long while, just an occasional grunt or muttered curse at a too-heavy pot. Soon, sweat is rolling down my back, so I push up my sleeves.

Just as I reach up for another sapling, Shelly grabs my hand. "What the hell is this?" she asks—suddenly, inexplicably angry. I glance over my shoulder, thinking I must have damaged one of the trees I unloaded, but then I realize she's looking at my arm. There are deep, angry bruises in the shape of fingerprints on my forearm, the bruised image of a large and powerful hand.

"I—I don't know," I stammer, taking in the damage. "It wasn't like this . . ." I trail off as I remember the sensation of being grabbed when I drove over the Lagerty border. The feeling of someone trying to yank me back.

"Who did that to you?" she asks.

"I don't know," I say. Shelly raises her thick, dark eyebrows.

"I mean . . . no one. I must have run into something," I

mumble. I pull my sleeve back down. "Looks like we're almost done here. I'm gonna go see if your mom needs help up front." I heave down one last potted tree before I walk away.

I know what Shelly's imagining—that some man has been yanking me around. That's all too common where I'm from. Hell, where anybody's from. She's probably imagining an abusive dad or an angry boyfriend. She doesn't know me well enough to know I've got neither.

It's just me. Just me and Granny and Daniel, which means it's just me.

Lula puts me to work pruning the plants in the greenhouse, which is a one-person job, so I get an hour to myself trimming dead brown bits off tropical plants with enormous fragrant blossoms and delicate lacelike fronds. Sweat drips into my eyes and makes my skin clammy, and after a while the smell of the flowers turns sickly sweet. By the time I finish, I'm dizzy and nauseous and have to stagger to the water cooler.

"You all right?" Lula asks, and I can see in her face that Shelly mentioned the bruises. Her eyes flit to my arms, even though my sleeves are covering them. She tilts her head slightly in concern.

"Just a little dehydrated, I think," I say between gulps of water. "I'll be fine."

"Take your lunch early, honey. There's an apple pie in the kitchen. Shelly made it." She gives me a gentle smile.

"Yes, ma'am," I say.

I'm halfway through a slice of pie when Shelly comes into the kitchen, dirt smudged across her forehead, her long curly ponytail over one shoulder.

"Good pie," I say around a mouthful. I swallow. "Wouldn't have figured you for a baker."

She gives me half a smile and pulls an enormous Tupperware container from the fridge and starts downing her lunch. Shelly eats every meal like it's the first one she's had in days and the last one she'll ever have.

"I'm sorry about earlier. I overreacted," she says, leaning down to cut herself a slice of pie. "It's just . . ." She clears her throat. "My dad was . . ."

I nod. "It's no problem."

For a few minutes, we make conversation about school and college, funny customers who've come into the store. It feels ordinary, easy, and for the first time in a long while I don't feel so alone.

The rest of the day passes faster than I'd like. I linger over my closing duties longer than I need to, finding fiddly little things I can pretend need done. But pretty soon I've run out of reasons not to go home. I say good night to Lula and Shelly, and I feel their concerned eyes on me as I walk back to my truck.

It's nearly five by the time I pull up the drive toward home. I put my foot on the brake beside the cemetery and let the truck idle while I think. Those fingerprints on my skin have me worried. But is it worse to face what made them or to put it off awhile longer?

I decide I'll at least go eat dinner and check on Granny. See if Daniel has fed that damn horse yet. Don't you owe more to the living than to the dead? Yet all the hairs on my nape stand on end as I drive by the gate, chill bumps running up my arms and torso.

Granny is right where I left her, peering down through her glasses at her arm, which looks worse than ever, yellow pus oozing from the sores. I'll bandage them tonight, but first I'll find Daniel and deal with him.

My cousin sits on the floor of his room, leaning against the bed rail, playing video games. He glances up at me, his eyes glazed.

"Did you feed Mountain?" I ask.

He shrugs.

"That horse is all you've got left of your mama," I say.

His expression remains blank, his eyes glassy. He's still stoned.

Daniel is a year younger than me, and his mother died last year. That's when he came to live here with me and Granny. We're a pair of orphans, or as good as. But he's sunk so far into grief or apathy or whatever it is that he's quit going to school. He won't even speak to me now.

That's what I've got for company out here. Worms and silence.

I've had enough of it. I lean behind the TV and yank a handful of cords from the wall. The screen goes black, but Daniel keeps hitting the buttons on his controller for a few seconds, as if he's on a delay. When he finally looks up, his eyes are so empty, it makes me shiver.

"Go feed your damn horse, Daniel, before I sell it for glue," I say, making my tone as mean as I can manage. The boy doesn't respond to gentleness.

He ducks his head and leaves the room, and I follow him to the front door to make sure he's heading to the barn.

"Daniel's doing bad, Granny," I say. "I think he might need help. More than I can give."

"Who?" Granny asks.

"Daniel, your grandson."

Granny bunches up her mouth, thinking. But I can tell she has no idea who I'm talking about.

"Your little Danny," I say. "Laura's boy."

"Melissa, when are you taking me to the doctor?" she asks, losing interest in the topic.

"In two days," I say, loneliness washing over me. I lean across the back of her chair to hug her neck. She gives me a single pat on my hand.

"Good girl," she says. "Good girl."

By the time I make dinner and clean the dishes, I'm exhausted. I think of the homework waiting in my bedroom, chapters and chapters of history, long sets of complicated equations, an essay on Cormac McCarthy.

I rub my arm where the phantom fingertips dug in. It hurts,

each fingerprint throbbing slightly. And I know what I have to do.

I go to the linen closet and pull down a heavy box from the top shelf. I carry it out to my truck and drive down to the cemetery. It's twilight, but it hardly looks different from this morning. The rain has stopped, but the sky is a sullen slate gray, no sign of stars. There's a cold breeze stirring the trees, setting the Spanish moss swaying. The moon is nearly full, but it's a low, indistinct haze of putrid yellow that gives no light.

Still, there's enough daylight left in between the drifting shadows for me to see the gravestones. I heft the box to my hip and open the creaky gate. The moment my foot touches the ground inside the cemetery, I can feel them. They churn around me like batter, responding to the beat of my blood, the warmth of my breath. They are cold and they are hungry, and I am life.

I think of all the places I'd rather be than here. Like with Shelly, on a date. Or even at the garden store with her, yanking down saplings from a truck. But this is where I belong, isn't it? Isn't this what it means to be born of the people who lie in this cemetery, born of the sweat and blood and soil of this town? Isn't *birth* just another name for *destiny*? Your family name the border between you and the rest of the world?

I try to take another step forward, but my ankle is held fast by invisible fingers. I bite back a yelp and kick my foot free.

More bruises for Shelly to wonder at tomorrow.

When I took over grave tending for Granny, she told me there wasn't anything to fear. She said the dead were memories, nothing more than the way a woman's perfume lingers in a room after she's gone. Grave tending helps them rest easier is all, she said, because they know they are loved, that they are not forgotten, even though their flesh rots in the ground, even though their bones lie cold and lonesome.

"Aren't they supposed to be in Heaven?" I asked her.

She smiled sadly. "They are supposed to be, yes, but some souls don't go easylike; some souls cling. But they are to be pitied, baby, not feared. Loved and cherished, not rebuked."

"Yes, ma'am," I'd said, though I wasn't sure I agreed with her. It seemed to me that a soul that preferred a cold grave to the white light of Heaven was suspect.

So I've always tended their graves with caution, kneeling in the dirt with my shoulders hunched and wary. Now I set down my box next to the most recent grave: Aunt Laura's, Daniel's mother.

She overdosed. A friend found her on the bathroom floor, suffocated by her own vomit. When she was young, she had dreamed of being a rodeo star, a champion barrel racer. She'd managed to keep a horse, even when she could barely feed Daniel, even when she lost him in the divorce.

I sing over her grave, a hymn about the resurrection, the promise of being embodied again, which is what the dead most want. As I sing, I clear away the dirty, broken bottles, the marred pennies, the tattered plastic flowers. I replace them all with fresh ones. Fake sunflowers, a tiny bottle of Jack Daniel's, freshly minted coins, and a little brown toy horse I found at Dollar General.

I move on to the next grave, my second cousin Sally, who I never met because she died before I was born. She'd been drinking and ran her car into a tree. No one was ever sure if she did it on purpose or not. Either way, her grave has always felt quiet to me, so I don't linger over her.

The grave I always take the most time on is Granny's mother's, Celine's, because Granny told me to. At first I thought Granny asked me to give her mother special care because she loved her, but every time I come out here I'm convinced otherwise. As I sing over her grave, the back of my neck prickles and my ears tingle, as if someone stands behind me watching. It's a heavy, oppressive feeling. I lay out two bunches of fake roses, a mini bottle of red wine, and a big handful of pennies. I sing an extra verse of the hymn over her grave.

But the oppressive feeling doesn't go away. If anything, it grows. My breath starts to come short, as if someone is siphoning the oxygen right out of my lungs. I stop singing and focus on my breathing, on pulling air in and forcing it back out. It feels like I'm breathing through a broken straw. Soon, I can't even stand.

I leave my box of grave tokens and crawl on my hands and knees back toward the gate. If I can just get out of the cemetery, maybe she'll let me go. But my vision is blurring and my chest feels like Mountain is standing on it. Panic surges through me, bone deep, marrow deep.

It must be my fear that wakens the rest of them.

Invisible hands pinch my skin and yank my hair and crawl beneath my clothes. Claws rake down the back of my calf, and I try to cry out, I try to scream, but there's no air in my lungs. I can't even sing to soothe them. I'm helpless, alone, and at their mercy.

I slump to the damp earth and hide my face in my hands while the ghosts assail me like a pack of crows, reaching out with their hungry hands to pick and peck and paw. *They're going to scoop out my organs*, I think, *They are going to drink the blood from my veins.*

And then I'll never make it past the mailbox, never make it past the city limit, never find out what else life might hold besides worms and silence.

"Melissa!" someone yells, and I pull my head up with agonizing effort. I blink, unbelieving, at Shelly. Shelly is standing at the cemetery fence, gripping the gate, silhouetted against the murky twilight sky.

I'm dreaming, I think, or maybe hallucinating from lack of oxygen. But she runs forward, and I feel her hands on me, so different from those of the dead. Her hands are warm and strong. She pulls me up off the ground, and holds me against her, saying something I can't make out. All I can do is stare at her and gasp, open-mouthed, like a caught fish.

She yells something and then picks me up and carries me, with effort, staggering through the cemetery gate. Her car idles in the grass, the driver's door open.

"You're having an asthma attack," I hear her say as she puts me in the car. She slams the door, and air rushes back into my lungs. I gasp it in with searing gulps that make tears stream down my face.

Shelly gets into the driver's seat and puts the car in reverse.

"Wait, stop," I manage to say with a hoarse voice. "I'm all right."

"You're not all right," she says fiercely, but she does stop.

I stare out the front window at the cemetery, which looks quiet and peaceful if you don't know any better. I wonder how I could possibly explain.

"Why are you here?" I ask her instead.

Shelly hesitates before she speaks. "I had a bad feeling. I tried to call you, but you didn't pick up. So I came to make sure you were all right."

"How do you even know where I live?" I ask, looking over at her.

Shelly bites her lip. "I went into your employee file to get your address. I'm sorry."

"You had a bad feeling?"

She nods. "I get them sometimes, and they won't let me rest."

"I don't have asthma," I say. I grasp for another explanation. "I guess it was . . . a panic attack."

Shelly's face hardens. "Why don't you come stay with Mom and me tonight?"

I think of Granny sitting in her chair with her tweezers, of Daniel staring vacant at a blank TV screen. "I can't," I say. "I'm needed here."

"In a graveyard at night?" she asks. "Who did this to you?"

I sigh. Shelly isn't from Lagerty. She wouldn't understand. "No one," I say.

"Melissa, look at yourself!" she snarls. She flips on the overhead light, and I see the damage the ghosts have done. Bruises all over my arms, my skin a tapestry of broken capillaries and red gouges. When I open the visor mirror, I wince at the sight of the bruises and scratches on my face and neck. I look like I've been beaten.

"I'm taking you to the hospital," Shelly says, backing the car away from the cemetery.

"No, wait, I—" Pain explodes in my belly and I double over. Shelly just keeps driving.

I can feel their hands inside me, tearing at me. I let out an agonized moan.

Shelly spins the car onto the drive and heads back toward the road, tires crunching gravel. She picks up speed, as if she can feel what's at our back.

I think I hear hoofbeats, which is probably only the frantic pounding of my own heart. But then Shelly swears and swerves, and I catch a flicker from the corner of my eye.

I turn my head, and there's Mountain, thundering beside us.

"Stop the car!" I yell, and Shelly slams on the brakes. I leap out and chase after Mountain, who bolts over the fence and into the trees, and runs full out, his sides heaving. He's going to crash into a tree and kill himself.

"Melissa!" Shelly yells. But I have to catch Mountain. It's Aunt Laura's horse, the last thing Daniel has of his mother. Daniel's been lazy about feeding him, but he'd miss him if—

Mountain vanishes. It's not that he goes out of my sight, so much as that he winks out, like a spent lightbulb. As if he were never there.

I stagger to a stop. The world feels suddenly unreal.

Shelly is beside me, her hand on my arm. "Why did you run?"

"Daniel's horse got out. Didn't you see it?"

She shakes her head uncertainly. "I thought there was something by the car, but . . ." She shakes her head again. "Is Daniel the cousin of yours who died? The one who lived in Georgia with his dad?"

"What? Daniel's not . . ." I was going to say he isn't dead, but suddenly I'm not so sure. I'm not sure of anything. "Can you drive me to the house?" I ask.

She crosses her arms. "How about the hospital instead?"

I huff out a frustrated breath. "I'm fine. I don't need it. It's just bruises."

"I'm not leaving you alone here," Shelly says. "I don't know what's happening, but I know it's not good."

"You can come in with me," I promise. And I want her to. I don't want to go in there alone. Because I'm not at all sure what I'm going to find.

Wordlessly, Shelly takes my hand and walks me to her car. She does a three-point turn and heads back toward Granny's house. When we pass the cemetery, her hands tremble on the steering wheel.

The horse pasture is empty. There's no Mountain standing tall and sullen at the fence.

My brain seems to buzz with flies as the house comes into view. "Pull over here beside the side porch," I tell Shelly. We walk up the long porch, its empty rocking chairs creaking as they move back and forth in the wind.

I open the screen door and then the kitchen door, and flip on the lights. The kitchen is clean and quiet, still smelling of dinner. But Shelly gasps and covers her nose and mouth.

We pass through to the back hallway and stop outside Daniel's door. I push it and the door creaks open. From the blue-tinged light coming in through the blinds, I see that Danny's room is the same as it was earlier. He's huddled under his covers.

"See?" I tell Shelly. "He's just asleep."

"Melissa," she says softly, almost pityingly. But there's fear in her eyes.

"What is it?" I ask.

"Look again," she says. She flips on the light, and reality reshapes itself around me. Daniel's room is empty. There are only a few cardboard boxes stacked against one wall. The air is musty.

I remember now. Danny died a year ago, just before Aunt Laura overdosed. She worried for weeks over his body being buried in a public cemetery, hundreds of miles away. She said his spirit would be lost and wandering.

I stagger backward into Shelly, who catches me with sure and gentle hands.

"I—I've heard stories about this town," Shelly says. "My dad was from here."

I take in the information, but it doesn't entirely register. Because I'm thinking of Granny in her chair in the living room, sitting under her lamp with a pair of tweezers, waiting for a worm to show itself beneath her skin. Dread pools in my gut.

"Have I ever mentioned my grandmother?" I ask Shelly.

"Melissa? Is that you?" Granny calls from the living room.

"Yes, ma'am," I call back by habit.

Shelly turns her head toward the living room. "Is that her?" she asks, her voice much higher than usual.

I nod. "She—she raised me," I say, needing desperately for Shelly to understand. "My mom dropped me off here one day when I was four and she never came back. It's been just the two of us since Papa died. And since Granny's arthritis got bad and her mind started to go, I've been taking care of everything."

"What about your dad?"

I shrug. "He doesn't matter. Granny said the only family you need is the family that stays."

"You ever think some of them stayed too long?" Shelly asks.

"What do you mean?"

"There're worse things than not being part of a family."

"Melissa?" Granny calls again.

"I'd better go check on her," I say.

"Come home with me," Shelly says, stopping me at the door. "Don't go in there."

"She needs me," I say, pulling away.

"Go pack a bag," Shelly says.

"Melissa?" Granny's voice has turned plaintive, querulous.

"You've stayed too long," Shelly says.

"Melissa?"

I turn to leave, but Shelly grabs my hand and holds it. "Don't go in there."

"What do you know?" I ask. "Is she——"

"Do you trust me?" Shelly asks, and I can feel her heart racing through our clasped palms. I study her face, her dark eyes, her set jaw. She's a stranger almost, but I do trust her.

I nod again.

"I'm telling you, Melissa, don't go in there. Just come home with me, please."

"Melissa?" Granny calls, and her voice cuts through me like

a blade. It hurts worse than all the bruises and scratches I earned in the cemetery. It aches in my heart, aches in my bones, in my marrow. "Melissa, baby?"

Tears start in my eyes and roll down my cheeks. "I'm coming, Granny," I say. I put my hand on the doorknob. I start to turn it.

"Melissa," Shelly whispers. "Don't. This doesn't have to be your life. Not anymore."

But it does, doesn't it? Because it's all I have.

I turn the knob and push the door open, just a crack. Shelly puts her hand over her nose and mouth and staggers away from the door, away from me. "Melissa," she gasps.

I stand frozen on the threshold, unable to go forward, unable to leave. I think about Mountain, winking out of existence. I think about Daniel's empty room.

"Melissa," Granny calls, her voice a sob. "Melissa, I need you. I need you."

I close my eyes. I think about the mailbox. I think about the city limits sign. I think about that highway that goes on forever. I think about where it might lead.

In one quick movement I pull the door toward me, slamming it closed. Granny weeps on the other side. It hurts so much, I cannot speak, not even to say goodbye.

I take Shelly's hand and let her lead me down the hallway and into the kitchen, out onto the porch, and back to her car. She guides me to the passenger side and shuts me in. We back out and start down the drive, gravel rattling beneath the tires, shadows pressing their faces against the glass.

Shelly holds my hand as we drive past the empty horse pasture and the darkened cemetery, as we turn onto the road, passing the mailbox. She holds my hand as we speed through town, past family cemeteries and rusting trailers and fields of cattle. She holds my hand as we pass over the town border and out of Lagerty.

She holds my hand as the dead claw and grasp at me, as their voices ring like bells inside my head. She holds my hand as Granny's cry fades into a whimper, as her body turns to rot.

She holds my hand as the dead sink back into their graves to dream.

She holds my hand as I leave them all behind.

The Tallest Poppy

by Chloe Gong

*E*VERY NIGHT, THE SEA SOUNDS LIKE IT'S MOVING CLOSER.
It doesn't matter how much I toss and turn and plug up my ears: The rushing water will grow to a crescendo and whistle through the gaps of the bedroom, bringing the smell of salt and brine into my blankets. I'll give up on sleep and lunge upright, hurrying frantically to the window as if this time—finally this time—I'll catch the sea in movement and find it to have invaded the beaches and risen up the hills, but the sea always stays where it is, its foamy edges crashing on the shore below, lit up by the glow of the moon.

I don't know how many nights of rest I've lost like this. I don't know how many nights it's been. They start to blend together, seamless at the stitches until I can't pull them apart anymore. Wave after wave after wave.

Sleep comes eventually. It is fought for. It is a beast that I chain up despite knowing it will tear free sooner or later, and I jerk awake again, disturbed by the rushing foam or the crowing morning birds or the house creaking.

There's only one method that works. I let the earsplitting noise break through. I let myself be pulled into the ever-nearing roar, eyes closed in the darkness, imagining the sea crawling and crawling until it pours into the old room and encases me whole.

Then I finally hear nothing, because I am swallowed underwater.

The lone house on the hills overlooking the beach is cursed, or at least that's what the townspeople say. I used to walk past this four-story structure every day on my way to school, though it always seemed a lot smaller when I was looking from the bottom of the long, ascending driveway. It's hard to deny that there are warranted reasons for the townspeople to claim the house is cursed. They mutter about how the elements must be excruciatingly loud so close to the beach, how there must be something wrong with the infrastructure if the family who lived there kept getting sick.

The first set of Abrams kids, Cammie and Louise, were in my year at school. At some point, their grandmother developed a lung infection, then their father caught a mysterious cough that ended with black vomit splashed on the walls of the local dairy. When they packed their bags for Auckland to go where the bigger hospitals are, they summoned their relatives to take over the house.

By chance, I sat next to Jason Abrams in English when his parents moved him into town and he started at our school. Nearing the end of the year he started to pick at his skin, opening different raw wounds inside his elbows each day, and he never came back after that summer. A new set of cousins moved in, but Alix and Neil were younger, so I only knew of them in passing. Last month, they were driven out too when their mum didn't wake up one morning.

She's not dead. Just mysteriously, continuously sleeping.

I come to a stop at the top of the driveway now, gazing down on the water. I breathe in. Breathe out. During this point in the summer, pollen dusts the air like a visible mist. I've gotten used to it—seventeen years living in the same tiny town will do that to a person—but there's something about being up so high that makes the suffocation feel more potent. All this greenery and color, blotted with intrusion. Flax bushes and waving stalks of Northland wildflowers that grow vertically, stretching as tall as a person before stopping abruptly. They spread in orderly clumps, bleeding down the hills until the dirt of the soil turns to sand and the sand washes into the frothy beaches.

The Abramses finally ran out of family members to take care of the house. A David Williams bought the property and moved in with his wife and three children last week, sending a ripple through the town, wondering where they came from. Yesterday I answered their poster seeking a live-in nanny for the summer. They hired me over the phone and asked me to come in immediately.

"Well," I mutter. "Doesn't look too cursed."

The house trembles under a gust of the salty gale. It doesn't matter how hot the temperature turns in the middle of the day: It's always brisk near the beach. From the driveway, I watch the second-floor windows shudder, then the front door open to bring out an old woman.

"Penelope Gao?" she bellows. "The new nanny?"

I hike my bag higher up on my shoulder and turn away from the water. When I walk toward the door, I'm trying my hardest not to shiver.

"You can just call me Poppy."

"This switch is for the dining room, but that one is for the bulb over the front door. Be careful which you're hitting, because if the door light is left on for too long, it'll overheat and burst."

I nod, taking mental notes while I follow Mrs. Fausse around. From the inside, the house is even more formidable. The floors stretch up to a height that feels a little dangerous when the wind blows hard, which was the first thing I noticed because I'm the one sleeping in their redesigned attic space, where a triangular window overlooks the downward slope of the hills.

"The front door gets sticky in the summers, so the last thing we need is to be trapped *and* groping around wildly in the dark."

Mrs. Fausse waves me down the third-floor corridor. She doesn't seem to mind how hard it is to walk here, feet sinking into the soft carpet with every step. When she opens the door to a playroom, we both cough, waving away the dust that explodes forward.

"The cleaner hasn't come in a while and big houses get dirty too fast," she says. "Makes my life hell."

I peer into the playroom, making a cursory inspection.

"You probably won't need to come in here often," Mrs. Fausse continues before I've finished looking, pulling the door closed. "The children have outgrown their dolls."

"But they still keep the playroom around?"

The kids are out with their parents at the moment, on some afternoon excursion through town, but dozens of photo frames around the house show me their grinning faces. Two boys around twelve and a little sister with her front teeth missing.

"Why not?" Mrs. Fausse proceeds down the hallway. "Did you graduate already, Poppy?"

The topic switch takes me by surprise. A beat passes before I hurry to follow, scrambling to remember how to answer. I almost say, *No, not yet.* A knee-jerk reflex from years of waiting. But it happened. I finished Year 13.

"Yeah, last month."

I got the early-decision full scholarship to my dream university half a world away. This summer I only need to make the money for the plane ticket out.

I can finally leave.

On the ground floor, Mrs. Fausse opens the back door. I follow her onto the deck, prepared to backtrack quickly like we did for the playroom, but the housekeeper stands where she is, hands on her hips, to gaze out at the scenery. The garden is enclosed with a man-made gate, but its natural landscape is part of the hills, no difference between the grasses on either side.

"There's the laundry line," Mrs. Fausse says, pointing. It takes me considerable squinting before I spot the metal structure in the garden, half hidden behind a large tree. On the other side of the tree, there's an old white man with a very white beard tending to the weeds around the trunk. He almost blends right into the garden too, as if he's an extension of the premises instead of a person of his own.

"I actually didn't know they were hiring a nanny until they brought you in." Mrs. Fausse walks back into the house, speaking over her shoulder. Everything in my sight is tinged with violet when I resume trailing after her, retinas seared by the brightness. "I guess this is a good way to spend a summer, hmm? When are you going to Auckland for uni?"

I blink, half in surprise, half to clear my vision. "Oh. No, I'm not going to Auckland."

"Ah, good choice." Mrs. Fausse pauses by the kitchen counter, sifting through the mail there. "My son went down to Auckland, but he came back a few years ago. It's so dangerous in cities. Too many people. Smaller is better."

"No, no." I wince, then wonder if it's worth correcting. "I'm going nowhere. No—I mean, overseas. I'm going overseas."

"Oh." Mrs. Fausse thinks for a moment. "Is that a good idea?"

She asks it without malice. The malice never comes until later. I have run this routine many times now. I can pick up the tune by ear and repeat every key on command.

"Leaving for *overseas*," Mrs. Fausse goes on, as if she has only misunderstood me and I'll correct her any second. "Why would you want that?"

Because I'm not content with one small corner of the world being all that I'll ever see. Because it is an ambitious person's nature to flock to where the world's beating pulse is. Because there should be no harm in admitting that the world's pulse is certainly not here, but I haven't once been able to say that aloud without the people around me thinking I'm looking down on them, and perhaps—God, deep down perhaps I am, but why

must I be punished for wanting *more*—

"I thought it would be fun," I answer. It's not a lie, at least. I'm sure it will be plenty fun to go somewhere with more than two Asian families, where I can't pause too long before interacting with townspeople I've never spoken to before, in case they assume I can't speak English in that split second.

"Well, I'm sure it will be." Mrs. Fausse shuffles the mail upright. "I think I hear the kids returning. Come meet them."

A few days pass before things start to go wrong.

There were the hints that started even earlier, I suppose. That prickle when I said hello to Beatrice and she grinned toothlessly, taking my hand to show me her crayon drawing. That thrum shooting across the thick carpet when I was sitting in the living room, scrolling through my phone while Connor and Leo were building a miniature train set on the kitchen counter. Easily ignored feelings of something being ever so off, but nothing that I would describe as strange.

They say the house is cursed. Still, people move in. Still, I believe that I'll be just fine.

I've always been the type to have too much faith in myself.

That night, the thump comes shortly after the clock ticks past eleven. I lift my cordless battery-powered lamp, eyebrows furrowing. Whether because of the wiring situation in the house or because the previous tenants didn't want light up here, there is no overhead bulb on my ceiling.

I walk to the attic door. Peer down the stairs onto the third floor. "Hello?" I call.

No response.

"Connor?" I guess. "Leo?" It's my responsibility to make sure the kids stay in bed and aren't wandering around during the middle of the night. Another thump sounds on the second floor, and with a sigh, I start down the stairs, the lamp still in my hand.

In the dark, every part of the house looks the same. My free hand runs along the walls in search of the light switch, but I'm not yet familiar enough with the house to know where they are without seeing them. I raise the lamp instead, as high as possible, and then—I sight a flash of movement over the banister onto the second floor.

A sudden coldness pinches my throat tight. That doesn't look like one of the kids. That looks like a fully grown person, standing upright, waiting in the dark.

For the love of God, *where* is the light—

My hand slaps down on a switch and a single bulb turns on above the stairs. It's dim . . . but it's enough to see that the mysterious figure is only Mrs. Williams, hovering on the second floor with a glass of water. An exhale tears through my lungs, relief flooding my senses.

"Mrs. Williams, you gave me a fright," I say, leaning on the banister.

She doesn't respond.

Perhaps the relief was too easily won.

"Mrs. Williams?" Slowly, I descend the stairs, my eyes pinned on her silhouetted form. Her pajamas are black from head to toe, which is why she blended right into the shadows without the light. By the time I'm standing right in front of her, she still hasn't stirred.

She must be sleepwalking. Her eyes stare forward at nothing.

I try not to startle her. I touch her elbow like one would touch a frozen deer, and when she turns to look at me—unhurriedly, blankly—I'm not sure if I have woken her at all.

"Are you okay?" I ask. "Would you like me to get Mr. Williams?"

"No need for that." She has answered my question, but somehow she doesn't seem like she heard it. "What are you doing here?"

"Here?" I echo. "I heard a sound, Mrs. Williams. I thought to check on it."

Mrs. Williams says nothing. She doesn't blink—and I count the seconds that pass by, *eight, nine, ten,* before her blond eyelashes gingerly flutter down once.

There's sweat gathering along my back.

"What are you doing *here*?" she asks again.

Here—the hallway? The house?

"I'm . . . I'm the nanny," I try, not sure what she's asking. "For the kids—"

Mrs. Williams turns away before I can finish. She climbs the stairs with languid speed, the glass of water in her hands splashing a small droplet over its side. I watch her disappear along the third floor, listen for her movement as her arms brush the walls.

It isn't until her bedroom door closes that I dare to move, returning to my attic room with a small tremor shooting down my spine. I set my lamp on the bedside table, then crawl under my blankets.

I don't think it's my imagination when I hear thumping again an hour later. This time, I don't go investigate.

The kids stay well behaved for the most part.

I begin to watch them with a fanaticism, wary that they'll do something weird the moment I have my back turned. What they could do, I don't know. But I've been on edge for weeks now, ever since the incident with Mrs. Williams.

It's none of my business if Mrs. Williams is sleepwalking and disturbing the foundation of the house, so I don't tend to her when I hear creaking past bedtime. Still—most nights it's not sounds inside the house that I hear but the rush of the sea outside, and I understand why the town gossips about people who willingly choose to live in a house like this. The sensation is overwhelming. I jerk awake in my sleep constantly, panicking that the water has washed up to my pillow. In the mornings, there's a tension behind my eyes that squeezes my skull if I move my sight too quickly from left to right.

Beatrice passes me a wooden horse to hold while she organizes the toys in the playroom. I clutch it readily, two hands around the legs like I'm protecting it from being stolen.

"You can put that over there, Poppy," Beatrice instructs seriously, pointing to a shelf of porcelain dolls.

"Yes, ma'am."

I drag myself up, blinking hard to clear the black dots scurrying across my vision. There's not long left of this job. A month more, maybe. Though the school year in town will start when summer ends in February, I won't be going anywhere until August, on the northern hemisphere's schedule.

I put the horse on the shelf, then frown, pushing the dolls tighter with one another to make more space at the end. *Is* it January? Or did we pass into February already? Have we celebrated the New Year? I can't remember. I need to check my phone later.

"What else?" I ask Beatrice.

She's eager to continue bossing me around, plucking up two Barbie dolls by their hair. "Hmmm . . . they're not pretty enough to sit with the others. We toss these out."

"What?" I hurry over and take the Barbies from her before

she can do anything rash. "They're perfectly good dolls. They'll look nice with . . ."

I trail off. The wooden horse I set on the lower shelf has fallen to the floor. It looks pathetic on its side, legs straight and useless. But the moment I lean to pick it up, a snap of wrongness flexes into my wrist.

My eyes snap up. I had cleared a segment of the shelf for the horse. Hadn't I?

Now the porcelain dolls are taking up the whole space again. Their beady eyes and painted smiles. There's a thin layer of dust on their fragile skin, as if the shelf hasn't been touched in years.

"Beatrice, did you pull the horse off?"

Beatrice toddles close, her nose wrinkled. "I was over there. Of course not." She pushes the dolls, then takes the horse from me and sets it back where it was. "There. They won't move now that I've done it."

A shiver dances along my neck. "What?"

Beatrice leans in. Cups two small hands around her mouth to funnel her whisper.

"The dolls don't like you," she says, as if divulging a deep secret. "They told me."

"What—" I don't know what comes over me. I huff, "Well, *I* don't like them either," and then I immediately feel ridiculous.

Down the hall I hear the rumble of Mrs. Fausse making the beds to prepare for Mr. and Mrs. Williams coming home from work. Beatrice is almost finished organizing her toys.

"Yell out if you need me, okay?" I scratch the inside of my elbow, making for the door. "I'm freshening up before dinner."

"Okey dokey," Beatrice says happily, sitting to play with the Barbies.

It'll all be worth it. I take the stairs up to my attic room, then close my bathroom door behind me. *You'll be out of here before long.*

I fill up the bathtub, perching on the edge while the water rises. The small window above the sink has been left open, bringing in a cold breeze that draws goose bumps on my shoulders when I fold into the scalding water. The sea is roaring at a thunderous volume. It must be high tide. Foam and seashells, crawling up the grassy hills and spitting sand into the soil.

I drop my head below the bathwater.

Enough. I don't want to hear it anymore. Stay back.

The sounds stop.

There was one morning in primary school when I overslept and neither of my parents knew I hadn't left the house yet. By the time I woke up and stumbled out of my room, the sun was so high up in the blue sky, hovering at its apex. I thought days had passed. I had only been displaced out of my routine, not the linear passage of time, but for the longest moment, I couldn't work past the overwhelming sensation. Cicadas going off in the distance, the sidewalk bright with reflected light, and me standing there—just standing there—looking around and thinking, *God,*

I'm not supposed to be here, I'm supposed to be somewhere else, this is wrong, this is wrong.

That feeling of displacement has been ringing in my head as one prolonged warning shriek since then. I keep waiting for it to stop, but there it remains, nestled in an unscratchable part of my body.

I exhale slowly, emptying my lungs. The bubbles blow into the bathwater, rising up to the surface. I don't move until my throat begins to burn and beg for air. Only then do I push up slowly, lifting my forehead from the water.

I can't go any farther.

I brace my arms, thinking I must have gotten snagged on some part of the tub, but then I try to sit and no—I'm being *held*, ten fingers clamped on my shoulders, squeezing . . .

Beatrice? Beatrice, this isn't funny. I CAN'T BREATHE, THIS ISN'T—

With one frantic surge, I break out from the water, spluttering.

"BEATR—"

I cut myself off as soon as my eyes fly open, hands gripping the sides of the tub. I'm alone. No trickster children anywhere to be seen. Only my own pruney fingers, clutching the tub so tightly that they are entirely bloodless.

When I lick my lips—a reflex—the tang hits my tongue immediately.

Salt. I'm tasting salt. Though the thought is preposterous,

I put my hand back into the bathwater, swirl it around, and lift it to my tongue again.

I rush out of the bath, flinging droplets over the tiled floors. I can't get out of the bathroom fast enough, pulling clothes on before I've entirely dried. In the bedroom I can still smell the sea's potent reek, so I hurry down the stairs—floor after floor—and burst out the back door.

The breeze makes it better. The breeze blows around my nose and sweeps away the feeling of being submerged in *seawater*, but when the beach is still right in the horizon, the suffocation comes back immediately.

I'm losing my mind. At night I can't sleep; now the daytime brings hallucinations.

"Getting dark out."

The voice makes me jump. It's accompanied by the sound of slashing metal, and I look down, peering over the deck to find the gardener with a pair of shears, snipping at the bushes around the house.

"The sun's setting earlier now," I reply. A white-hot ember, hovering above the water like a fragment of a lolly. It'll melt into the waves, sink sludge into the dark blue and settle to the bottom of the ocean bed. "Please excuse me."

The gardener says nothing in reply. I only hear his shears, echoing twice when they snap shut, once to follow me into the house and a second time to whisper a warning.

The sea is moving closer.

I know this as I know my own name, as I memorize unshakeable facts. Three times nine is twenty-seven, the planet Venus spins clockwise, the sea moves closer every night.

I lift onto one elbow. The clock shows two in the morning. Somewhere on the third floor, I hear a thump. Then it comes again, persistently, and I swing my legs out of bed.

"Mrs. Williams again?" I murmur under my breath. This time I don't bring my lamp with me. I know where the light switches are and the moon has been bright enough these last few days to light my way, streaming in through the windows at the end of the hall. At first I turn the corner and assume that Beatrice is lying in the hallway. I blink, then realize the shape isn't Beatrice; it's her porcelain dolls, arranged in a tight circle.

They turn to look at me.

I'm dreaming, I think. I must have fallen asleep without knowing.

I inch a step closer. Something about the sight is so absurd that my initial instinct is not fear, it's incomprehension. Cursed house or not, there is a vast difference between mysterious sicknesses and dolls that come alive. There must be marionette strings here, moved by a careful hand. That's the only explanation.

The moment I reach out to find the strings, my fingers brush against something. I wasn't imagining it—the dolls are being held up with thin string, barely visible in the dark. When I give one a pull, however, my wrist smarts with an immediate needle-prick twinge.

I flinch, drawing my arm back. Stare at the smooth surface of my skin, unable to believe what I am seeing.

More string. The barest inch, sticking out from inside my wrist like a vein that grew astray.

"What the hell?" I whisper.

"Don't." The voice is faint. I could say I am imagining it. Or it could be coming from the doll to the far left, with the ruffled pink dress.

"I have to." I pull the string; as easily as a knife through soft butter, it glides open a red line from my wrist to my elbow. The sting is fierce and piercing, but I bite back my hiss. Where is the end of this string? How deeply is it buried?

"Stop pulling." Another one of the dolls—possibly, doubt-fully, certainly. "You'll kill yourself."

"Shut up." I say it to myself. I say it to the dolls. "I won't have this inside me." I won't be connected to a set of strings. I won't be made into some plaything.

"It's not harming you."

"I need to *leave*."

The dribble of blood starts in earnest, smearing along my fingers, dropping rapidly onto the carpet. I've pulled the string up to my shoulder. It gives no indication of ending.

"No one ever leaves." That's a new voice, a lower timbre—the doll in the yellow dress.

"Why are you hurting yourself just to leave?" Another voice. Farther away. The doll in the corner. "Do you think you're *special?*"

With a cry, I let go of the string. Tears spring to my eyes and I'm heaving for breath, unable to bear the searing pain when the incision reaches my neck. There's a panic constricting my lungs, wondering if one wrong twitch is going to cut a line right across my throat. But maybe . . . maybe if I give it one more yank. Maybe the end is somewhere nearby, requiring but one last gasp.

"Shut up," I spit again, closing my fingers around the string. "You don't want me here anyway! You don't like me!"

"Outsider!" they start to crow. I've encouraged them. Their voices clash together, echoing and echoing down the hallway as if the walls are made of cavernous stone instead of soft plaster and wood. "Leave then! See if we care!"

I pull. There's so much blood that my grip is slippery, slick against my burning skin. I'm delirious. I'm in agony. "I'm *trying*—"

"No, don't!" The green-dress voice hushes the others. "You can't leave. You can never leave. You're ours now!"

"*Enough*—"

Just before I can find the end of the string, a flare of light beams to life overhead, and I'm so startled by the brightness that my hands fly to my eyes, flinching. One moment the smell of metal pervades my every sense; the next, nothing. I suddenly get the impression that I've been dropped into a new room, and though I know I remain unmoving, I lower my hands carefully, wondering if I will emerge in new surroundings.

It's still the hallway. But no dolls, no peeling skin, no deep incision from my wrist to my neck, torn apart by a buried string.

"Poppy, is that you?"

I twist around. Mr. Williams is standing at the other end of the hallway, a frown on his face.

"There were dolls," I say quietly. "Dolls everywhere."

For a moment, Mr. Williams only blinks. Then: "Dolls? Bea's dolls?"

It starts to register how I must sound. Like someone still caught in the throes of sleep, raving about the last nonsensical thing I had seen. My legs are shaking when I rise to my knees. I scrub at my wrist, but I can't find the slightest trace of a cut nor the phantom impression of string.

"I must have been sleepwalking."

"Off to bed, then," Mr. Williams says nicely.

I nod. I don't dare look in the reflection of the windows when I walk past him, afraid that I'll see the weeping gouge I cut across my throat.

The house is cursed, they have said so all along.

I nick myself slicing apples the following day. I get my hair caught in the laundry line the next, then trip on the stairs the afternoon after that. Other events follow. Lights turn on automatically when I walk into a room. Electrical faults, maybe. The bathroom heating rumbles to a start when I take a shower, easing itself off the moment I leave. Pipe malfunctions, maybe. Occasionally I think the kitchen drawers might be shuffling around when I'm not watching, opening and closing at random. I could blame a stray breeze, I could blame Beatrice's fast hand . . . or I could accept the strangeness.

I begin to imagine the house communicating with me directly in a push and pull: It wants me out desperately; it wants me to stay just as badly. Hurt me, scratch me, hurl terrible words that mark my skin; then embrace me, claim me, demand that I take it for my own and never leave it.

I wander around the living room, hands trailing across the cabinet. Even though Mrs. Fausse cleaned this morning, I cut five lines through the thin layer of dust that has gathered on the surface. I am not scared by a mere house. I have no interest in admitting defeat and fleeing. Once I finish the job, I'll walk away with my head high. Besides, it's not like I'm going anywhere until I've taken my last paycheck. I need that plane ticket.

"Poppy, look at what I can do!" Leo rolls up a wad of wet paper and hurls it at the wall, making it stick in a clump.

I roll my eyes. "Oh, and now I have to clean it up?"

"It's *art*."

"Let me get a bucket before you ruin the carpet." I turn on my heel, intending to make for the adjoined kitchen. Instead I almost spring three feet into the air when I find Mrs. Williams under the hallway arch, watching me blankly.

"Goodness, don't be startled," she says, a smile transforming her expression. "I'll get the bucket. Poppy, is this your last week?"

Given her question, she wants me to follow. I scramble after her into the kitchen.

"Yes. Until Friday."

Mrs. Williams leans down to open one of the cupboards. "I have a proposal, then. How would you like to stay until August?"

The house creaks under my feet. The floorboards groan, complaining loudly and whispering excitedly in the same breath.

"What?" I say aloud.

"Well, you're here until then, aren't you?" Mrs. Williams continues. "Goodness knows why you're leaving after that, but there's plenty of time before August. The kids enjoy your company. Who knows, maybe you'd like to stay longer for a permanent position."

Definitely not, I think. But there's no harm in more money, is there?

"I'll think about it," I answer. "Can I let you know on Friday?"

"Of course."

Mrs. Williams slams the cupboard closed, the sound as decisive as a car wreck.

The kids are at a playdate on Friday, so there's not much for me to do except mosey around the halls and muse about Mrs. Williams's offer. I wonder if the house has calmed down in its attempts to play with me.

The sun is setting. When I go up to my room, the walls are enswathed in shadow, swallowed by the purpling gloom outside.

I can hear the sea. In the growing dark, sound booms louder than anything else, wave after wave smacking against the sand and climbing the hills.

Despite my indecision, I did pack already. I only brought a small backpack of stuff anyway; it would be easy to take everything out again if I do choose to stay.

"It wouldn't be so bad," I say aloud. I fold onto the bed. Lie onto the pillows. "It's only another few months."

At some point I fall asleep. A very brief nap—no more than ten minutes pass before the crash of a wave wakes me up again, but by then night has fallen fully in my room, impossible to see even my hands in front of me.

I stretch to turn on the lamp. When its glow illuminates my

bedside, I become aware that there's a heavier presence upon my blankets, something that wasn't there before.

I don't turn to look first. I stretch my hand back—one inch then another—and when my fingers hit something cool, something like porcelain, I know exactly what has found its way near me.

What am I doing? I think suddenly. Another few months will turn into a year. A year will turn into a decade. I can't stay here forever. I won't.

In a lurch, I shove the porcelain doll away and let it hit the floor with a shattering sound, uncaring that it has broken. The little hairs at the back of my neck stand ramrod straight, as if I had woken up in a bed full of maggots instead, as if the doll's beady eyes are eggs waiting for their moment to burst. There's no time to dawdle. While the house is quiet and unoccupied, I pick up my packed bag and haul it high on my shoulder, hurrying down the stairs. I don't want to see any of the Williamses on my way out. Some part of me believes that if they see me en route, they will not let me leave.

"Almost there, almost there, almost there." The words slip from my mouth like a prayer mantra, used like a length of rope to pull myself along. My heart thunders an echo to my footfall.

I tug the front door. It won't budge.

The front door gets sticky in the summers, Mrs. Fausse's voice echoes from a lifetime ago. I pull again, panic rising in the heat of my throat, but the more desperate I grow, the harder it is to secure a proper grip, and I turn on my heel, making for the back door instead.

It pushes open easily. The sweet tang of relief is overwhelming on my tongue, mixed with the biting salt air.

But it is dark. And when I attempt to leap off the deck and exit through the garden, I misstep, landing among the bushes instead, air blowing out of my lungs with a curse.

My hand flails up, desperate for some sort of hold. I only find a rosebud to grab—useless. A thorn presses into my finger; I hiss and let go. The laundry line creaks with the wind. It blows once, spinning ninety degrees.

"Get up," I huff. "Come on."

My bag is deadweight. I try to shake it off my shoulder, but I only get caught deeper in the tangle of branches and thorns. I feel as though I am locked in a dream: my limbs heavy and cumbersome and unwilling to cooperate. Time moves in a bizarre sort of way while I try to regain my senses. I twist and nothing responds right. I open my mouth to yell for help and not a sound comes out.

I am another one of the flowers, rooted down in the bush.

A sound echoes through the garden. At first I think it must be the laundry line again, but it is sharper: metal sliding across metal. It comes again, closer. The glow of the moon has started over the horizon.

"Wait," I gasp. I strain my eyes, my ears, struggling to

understand why I cannot move, struggling to gauge what is approaching nearer and nearer. When a lull between waves hushes the beach and leaves the garden quiet, I finally understand.

I tip my head up and see the gardening shears pulled wide above me, two hands on either side, ready to close the blades down.

"Can't have any overgrowth," the gardener says.

"Stop," I croak. I close my eyes. "I only wanted—"

Snip!

The sea arrives.

When it washes up the hills, it swallows the offshoots and limbs that have been neatly trimmed from the bushes, devoured right into the foam like the excess never existed. When it washes around the house, it fades as quickly as it had come, purging out the nooks and hollows so that they are uniform once more.

Neat as a picture, a garden with not a poppy out of place.

Loved by All, Save One

by Tori Bovalino

WHEN WE WERE YOUNGER, WE USED TO GO SEARCHING FOR HER. Lee and Jase and me, the three of us in thick rubber boots coated with mud, armed with Jase's paintball guns like we were playing at war. Before we all grew up, before the Friday nights in my basement watching movies turned into sneaking warm six-packs into the fields, drinking at the bonfires after darkness fell, it was the three of us and our ghost. Before we changed—or maybe, before we became ourselves.

We used to go searching for her, the ghost who haunts these woods and quite possibly my house, too. Now, instead of searching for specters, we're scavenging for beer and liquor in my basement when my parents go away. Like tonight, when Mom and Dad are on some trip to Chicago to promote their supplement business.

My parents did a major swerve (or went through a midlife crisis) when they quit their jobs two years ago to become fitness influencers. First they overhauled the basement and then the detached garage, discarding the paint cans and old tools and creating a sleek gym. Then came the endless filtered pictures and videos for Mom's Instagram and then their YouTube channel. The weirdest thing is, it actually *worked*. All of the gym tutorials and product placements led to a full-blown supplement company, as unlikely as that was in a place like small-town Pennsylvania.

I don't fully understand the whole thing, if I'm being honest. All I know is that since they started it, our basement has had less alcohol and more gym equipment. Lee, Jase, and my searches have become more extended and less fruitful.

"Where do you think they buried her?" Jase asks from behind the boiler. I don't know why he's searching for anything back there—Fireball doesn't literally require any heat—but hey, I'm not one to question his methods. Perhaps it's a good hiding place, since the boiler wouldn't show up in any of my parents' videos. The last time one of Mom's fans spotted alcohol in the background, they had hate comments from internet randos for weeks about the effects of drinking on fitness. "Like, the first time."

Neither Lee nor I have to ask who he's talking about. It's always Barbara. She's like the unspoken fourth member of our group, though none of us has seen her in real life. Barbara Davidson.

If the legends are to be believed, she was killed here, in my house, in the 1800s. Decapitated by someone who broke in when she was watching the homestead in her parents' absence. Body buried under the floorboards. Head was never found, murder was never solved, etc., etc.

And if the further stories are to be believed, she's haunted this place ever since: her headless body here, in my house and the woods surrounding; and her head in weird, inexplicable places in Darlington. I used to wonder about that when I was lying awake at night, a child at an impressionable age, thinking of ghosts. Which side got her consciousness? Her brain, and whatever memories we take into the afterlife? Assuming ghosts do that, that is.

Assuming ghosts exist.

"Up your asshole," Lee says.

I shoot him a glare because it's funny when we're talking about keys and decidedly less so when we're talking about murdered people.

Lee has given up the search for vices. He stretches out on the couch, body too long to actually fit, feet dangling off the end. Lee isn't popular—none of us are—but he's definitely the one with the most game. Girls at our school don't shoulder past him in the hallway, don't ignore him like they do Jase and me. People listen when Lee talks.

Even if 99 percent of what comes out of his mouth is totally inappropriate.

Jase emerges from behind the boiler. He sneezes, sending a cloud of dust flying from the top of the boiler. I realize that I've been looking at Lee for too long—not in, like, a longing way, considering I'm not really interested in guys. Perhaps it's more like I want to become him. I want to peel his skin away and find out how he is the way he is, how he convinces people to like him. It's a subtle magic trick with Lee, one I can't quite understand. I practice his smile sometimes when I watch myself in the mirror, but it doesn't work on my face, doesn't match my braid and flannel shirts like it does Lee's lean, boyish face.

"What are we gonna do?" Jase asks. He's looking at Lee too, even though we're at my house. When push comes to shove, we always cede to him.

He shrugs, so I shrug, and the three of us look at each other. There isn't much *to* do. The only thing still open is Eat'n Park in Chippewa, and it's been snowing since noon, so the roads are shit. Plus, Jase hates driving in the snow, and my car can't really handle it, and my parents hate when I take the truck when they're not home.

Lee shoots me a desperate glance. "What do you think, J?"

He's called me J for as long as we've been friends, which is basically since our moms met at a church baby group. He calls Jase J too, so it's not like it's a cutesy thing. A darker part of me wonders if he knows my name at all, or if J is just his way of relegating Jase and me to his sidekicks. And then I feel terrible for those thoughts because, at the end of the day, Lee is the nicest person I know.

Besides, at least he doesn't call me Jenny. As far as nicknames go, J is the most comfortable shortening of Jenna I've heard.

"There's nothing to do," I say. But that's a pointless statement. There's never anything to do here in our corner of Pennsylvania. And we don't need alcohol to have fun, but it does spice things up.

"She could've been buried right here," Jase says, continuing the discussion that he might've been having with himself in his own head. He kicks the ground with one of his steel-toed boots. It's cement underneath the carpet.

"This basement didn't exist in the 1800s, dipshit," Lee says.

He's right, but our house was built right over the footprint of hers, so I'm not sure it matters.

"We could tell ghost stories," I say, pulling at the rolled sleeves of my flannel.

But Jase makes a face. "They're all old and boring anyway. You sure you don't have a stash somewhere?"

I'm chewing on my lip, thinking it over, when I remember that my great-uncle slipped me a bottle of peach schnapps at New Year's that we've yet to tap into.

"Be right back," I say, already darting up the stairs. They creak under me. Our house has enough of a general haunted house vibe on its own, what with the age and surrounding woods. The literal murder on these grounds certainly doesn't improve things.

I dash through the main hallway, past the darkened, empty

rooms, and up to the second floor. I didn't turn on any lights before we went to the basement, and now that the sun has gone down, it feels ominous and awful and ten degrees colder. This is why Lee and Jase stay with me when my parents go away: It's just too fucking creepy to be here by myself.

It's funny, how our house really is versus how it looks in my mom's glossy YouTube videos. There is always a plethora of full-strength lights to illuminate the clean surfaces and artsy décor. They put a lot of money into the house when her channel took off and people started noticing the walls and cabinets as much as the yoga poses and recipes. But even with all that improvement, it's old and empty and creaking and dark.

The upstairs hallway isn't much better, so I hightail it to my room at the end. The twinkle lights I put up last summer are on whenever I'm home, so at least this part of the house doesn't feel awful. It takes me approximately 0.3 seconds to recover the schnapps from the bell of my saxophone, but I'm not quite ready to go back through the house again.

I lean against the window and look out at the snow. It's fallen thick, fresh and glimmering under the moon. When we were kids, we would've loved a snowfall like this. Lee and Jase and I would've spent ages sledding and building snowmen. There's something bittersweet about this, about how we've stayed in the same place but left all those old things behind. I grip the neck of the schnapps bottle tighter in my hand. I hate this sometimes, this playacting at adulthood when we're still just kids. Maybe I still want to go out and play in the snow.

"JENNAAAAAAAAA!" Lee calls from the basement. "VODKAAAAAAA!"

I don't know if this means he's found vodka or he wants vodka, but either way, I can't stay up here and be grumpy all night. I'm feeling odd, and I can't quite put my finger on why. Perhaps it's because it's my last winter here, in this house, and I still haven't met our ghost. And perhaps it's because this might be the last night the three of us are like this, bored and young and restless, locked in my house overnight by snow and circumstance.

I plug my phone into its charger in my room and start back down toward the boys. There's a heavy sense of dread in the pit of my stomach, even though I'm not alone in the house, even though the boys are downstairs to keep me company. When I was younger, I used to dare myself to take every footstep down the long, creepy hall. I used to tell myself stories, to promise myself that nothing could hurt me in my house. After all, it's *mine*.

Not Barbara's. Not any ghost's.

I have that feeling again now as I creep down the hallway. I grip the neck of the bottle and peer into the gloom at the end of the hallway, toward my parents' room. They left their door open, and the doorway is a gaping maw of darkness. I don't like it, but it feels too childish to redirect just to close it.

Something creaks downstairs.

If I wasn't hyperfixating, I don't know if I would've noticed. But I am, and I do—it's not Lee and Jase in the basement, because this is a wood creak or a door creak. I've lived in this house my whole life. It's not the wind or any sort of shifting.

Someone is moving in the house.

I tiptoe around the stairs and pause on the first one, listening. There are footsteps on the wood floor, downstairs, at the other end of the house. I think they're coming from the living room.

It could be Jase or Lee—but no, because I can just barely hear the murmur of their voices, still in the basement.

Perhaps, in all my thinking of *her*, I've summoned her. Willed her into existence. Perhaps from whatever plane she occupies when she's not fucking around in the mortal world, Barbara decided to pay us a visit.

My heart is pounding. Lee laughs raucously at something downstairs, and all I can hear are the footsteps growing louder.

If it is a ghost, no matter what connection I think we may have, I can't face her alone. I creep down the stairs, focusing on the sound of those footsteps. They halt for a moment and I'm wondering if I imagined it when I hear it: thumping. I can't figure out where it's coming from, but something tells me it's dangerous. A chill runs down my spine.

Can a ghost actually harm me?

I'm convinced that I'm going to turn the corner at the end of the stairs and see her, headless and shadowed, silhouetted in the dark hallway. And when that happens, when I see her . . . I don't know what I'm going to do. My heart might actually beat out of my chest.

I wish oddly for those paintball guns we used to carry around the woods, hunting ghosts.

I turn the corner. There's no ghost. It's completely, totally empty and dark, the window outside showing the same spread of snow I could see from my window upstairs. Except—

Except there are footprints. Fresh ones.

Leading to the house.

I freeze, staring out at them.

We don't have neighbors. In the technical sense, Lee is my neighbor, even though his house is two miles down the road. Our old house is surrounded by woods in all directions, and our driveway takes a full minute to access on a good day.

My point is, you can't just *stumble* upon my house. And Dad had our address taken out of the phone book last year, after my mom had a run-in with an internet stalker and he got a weird bit of fan mail with some dude's toenails sealed inside in the same week.

But someone has found my house, or Jase or Lee went outside, and that's not a thing, because I can still hear them. But I also hear the creaking in the living room.

There is, quite possibly, someone else inside my house.

I'm halfway down the hall when Jase rounds the corner

from the kitchen clutching a bag of chips. Maybe he was who I heard moving around, coming upstairs for snacks. "Jenna? Shit, I thought I heard you in the other room. Did you find it?"

I round the corner and press a finger to my lips. He's there, in the hallway, lanky as ever. This is why Jase and I can't get girls: We both look like our limbs are the wrong size for our bodies, like there was too much drinking going on in the good ol' human factory when our parts were tossed together.

He frowns at me. I can barely read his face in the darkness.

"There's someone outside," I whisper to him as quietly as I can. "I saw their footprints."

Jase glances over his shoulder. At what, I don't know. "Where?"

"From the hall window."

His eyes flick over my head. He squints a bit, and creeps down the hallway, passing me. To the front door, I realize. His fingers are trembling when he flips the lock.

"Should we call someone?" I ask.

"Let's just make sure it's not—"

Downstairs, someone turns on music and I nearly jump out of my skin. But as soon as the beat picks up, we recognize Lee's favorite country song. I feel like my heart is in my throat. I pat for my phone to call my parents, but I left it upstairs.

Footsteps sound on the front porch, even louder than the ones in the other room. Jase is still hunched by the door, and his eyes are wide as he looks at me. We don't have windows near the door—I can't see onto the porch. I can't see if someone's there, if I'm imagining it. Lee's honky-tonk music from downstairs is actually going to rupture my skull.

Someone rattles the doorknob, and I clap a hand over my mouth before my scream gets out. Jase shuts his eyes tight, bringing his knees to his chest and curling around them. I somehow manage to knock the schnapps bottle off the step next to me and it rolls down the stairs, not breaking, but landing against the front door next to Jase's leg with a thud.

I am eternally grateful to him for locking the door.

My breath catches in my throat. What do I do? What do I do? What the hell am I supposed to do? If I run, go downstairs, or out the back door, I lose track of where the person on my porch is. But if I stay here . . . if I stay here and he gets in . . .

A dragging sound and another thump. Not on the porch, but inside, the sounds I heard earlier, coming from the back door and my mom's studio, and it doesn't matter because *they're already inside my house.*

Basement, Jase mouths at me. I nod. He goes first and I follow and together, we run.

The story goes, she was just home by herself, keeping an eye on the homestead. Feeding chickens and cows as her parents went to Pittsburgh for livestock. Maybe she had a baby. Maybe she was divorced. Maybe she was widowed, or she'd left her husband.

The details of her, her personal life, her wants and dreams and desires, are all lost to time.

Her murder, really, is all that remains.

She was alone in the house when someone broke in. When I was younger and impressionable, I used to imagine her on that night. Maybe she locked the door—if that was even something they did in those days. Maybe she had a book and a candle and she was reading in bed, thankful for her nice house and loving family, thankful that she had her health.

I wonder if she saw his face, the face of her murderer. In darker times, I wonder if she was still alive when he cut her head off, or if she was already dead by then. For her sake, I hope she was.

Most of all, I wonder if she's caught in that. The endless loop of pain, of misery, of loss. I wonder if, through the centuries since her death, she haunts this place because she knows it could happen just as easily all over again.

"Let's get Lee and get out," I whisper breathlessly. I'm trying so, so hard to hear where they are, to monitor the crunch of snow if someone is going around the house. "Do you have keys?"

He nods. I want to grab his arm or hand, to reassure myself that we're going to be okay, but the truth is, I'm too terrified to even consider what happens next.

When we get to the basement stairs, we realize that, for some reason, Lee has turned the lights off. Jase and I exchange a look.

He flips the switch. Nothing happens.

I swallow hard.

"Where's the fuse box?" Jase asks, probably thinking the same thing I am.

"I don't know." I really have no idea. Jase grabs my hand.

In the dining room, glass shatters. I shriek, the sound ripping out of me before I can stop it, and Jase drags me down the stairs and shuts the door behind us, throwing the lock. He somehow manages to turn his flashlight on and the shaft of light illuminates the shapes of the basement.

"Lee!" I yell. I don't care if the guy upstairs hears. We have to get *out* of here. Jase and I are running toward the back door, calling for Lee, when Jase trips. He takes me down and we both go sprawling. I hit my chin hard on the ground and find myself in a pool of something warm and sticky, smelling of copper.

Blood.

Beside me, Jase is gagging. "Lee!" he shouts, aiming the flashlight. I can only just see him: the glassiness of his eyes, his slack mouth, the smashed-in side of his head.

Footsteps sound in the darkness. Not upstairs, but down here. With us. A shadow moves closer until I can see him: a big dude in a ski mask. He holds a knife. His knees pop as he crouches down to look at us.

"You weren't supposed to be here," he says.

Save me, I think. What else is there to do? Who else is there to call on?

After she was murdered, her body was shoved under the floorboards of her house. Her family came back to find no trace of her. I wonder if there was blood, or if there was just nothing— but again, historical records are sparse on those details.

They didn't know what had happened to her until days later, when the smell started. They pulled up the floorboards to find her body there, mottled flesh in the summer heat. They never found her head.

When they buried Barbara, I imagine they thought they were setting all of it to rest. This woman, her life cut short for no reason, her pain, her suffering.

But she lingered. She's here in this house, in these woods. And I whisper her name over and over again, a prayer, as if that will save me when nothing else can.

They blindfold us and lead us away from the house and into the woods. Tie us up, both of us on either side of Lee's sagging body, a tree at our backs. Lee is not breathing. I know this as a fact, but I am unable to connect that fact with the reality of what it means.

It's cold. My eyelashes are frozen together with tears that won't fall, soaking the blindfold.

The bigger one of the two pulls our blindfolds down to gag us. Neither of us even tried to scream when they dragged us from the house—it's useless. The wind is howling loud through the trees, and anyone who heard us would assume it's another frozen gust.

There is no running from this.

And Lee is . . . Lee is . . . No. I cannot admit it, cannot even think the words, even as his body grows colder and colder against mine, unable to retain heat in the winter chill.

We have no phones, no weapons, no escape plans. Jase is bleeding from his forehead—one of them knocked him on the head when he tried to scramble as we were dragged out of the basement—and I can't even feel my fingers or toes anymore. My mouth is full of blood from biting my tongue when I fell. All I can do is swallow it down.

The two men are talking in low whispers a little ways from our tree. I can only hear snippets of conversation: They didn't intend for us to be here; they didn't plan for something like this.

We knew too much. And they'd already . . . Lee. They'd already hurt Lee.

They could not leave us alive.

I turn my head, trying to catch Jase's eye over Lee's head. He's staring straight ahead, his mouth slack, eyes distant.

I swallow another mouthful of blood. My parents will come home to find us gone and suspect we were at Lee's or Jase's or somewhere else in town. Hours will pass, then days. Maybe they'll find our bodies out by the river after the snow thaws come spring. Maybe we'll be reduced to ash.

There's a high, keening sound, stifled by the gag. It takes me a moment and a frantic look from Jase to realize that the sound is coming from me.

We are going to die.

"Hey!" one of them yells. He's pulled a knife from somewhere. "No sound. I'll kill you if you make another noise."

As if they aren't going to kill us anyway.

A prayer or an invocation, I think her name over and over again. Barbara. Perhaps it's this land that's cursed, stained with blood, wrecked.

In hypothetical lunchtime conversations, rehashing movies and true crime documentaries, we always say we'll fight back. That it's weak and foolish to let yourself be bested, to let yourself be killed. As if it's the victim's idea to become a victim.

But I have no fight in me here, tied to a tree in the bitter cold.

They have knives and warmth and energy and strength over us. We're three kids, hoping against hope that our parents will come home early, that someone will come to our rescue.

I'm still thinking about this, wrists rubbing raw against my restraints, when the fog creeps over us.

It's not uncommon to have fog in our corner of the world, but it doesn't come like this: creeping in tendrils, wrapping around the trees like it has intent. And it definitely doesn't thicken into a column, a shape. The form of a headless woman appears in the space between the intruders and us.

She's dressed in old clothes, a colorless dress and an apron. The collar of the dress is stained dark. Her neck ends in a ragged lump just above her throat. The woman's hands are stained with blood too, like they'd been at her throat when her head was removed.

Even without eyes, without a gaze, I get the impression that she *sees* us. Something cold nudges against my hand. It's Jase's fingers, just as frozen as mine. I look over to see the unrestrained fear in his eyes.

We were not searching for her this time, not turning over all the legends and calling for her ghost. Her name was Barbara in the time when she lived. She was a woman who would've been otherwise forgotten by history if it weren't for the brutality of her death.

Over two hundred years ago, she'd been killed in my house, her body ruined and crumpled and left to rot. Over two hundred years ago, her personhood had been stripped from the record and she'd become a haunt, a ghost, a warning.

Now, in the woods behind the place she died, she stands, nearly corporeal. Fury rolls off her in waves—impossible to explain, but I know that Jase feels it too. She faces us for a moment longer, taking in the three of us, and then turns toward the intruders. They're frozen in place, slack-jawed, staring. If they hadn't expected us, then they surely hadn't expected a ghost.

The restraints around our wrists and ankles slacken. They're just ropes, taken from my dad's workroom. Something hot flares against my wrist. I stare down at my ankles incredulously: The ropes are *burning*, smoking and blackening, then falling away.

Someone screams. It's the bigger intruder, his veins going purple and blood dripping from his mouth. He's gripping his throat, like something's choking him. Barbara moves closer to them. The other one watches his companion for a moment, sees the ghost approaching, turns on his heel, and runs.

I lose sight of him for a second. The first man's throat explodes in a flash of blood, the droplets forming a haze in the frozen air.

"We have to *run*," Jase says, his hand locking on my upper arm. But I'm still frozen to the spot, watching the specter move over the frozen land. The bigger intruder crumples, blood and other bodily matter leaking onto the snow and slush around him.

The ghost is moving toward the back of the second intruder, who is scrabbling over roots and ice to get away from us.

Jase lays out Lee, searching for a pulse, but it's useless. The wound on the side of his head is too big, red and ridged with bone and gelatinous inside things that I'm trying not to look at too hard. I think it might be his brain, and if I look, I will vomit and I will not make it through to whatever we need to do next to survive after this. He was probably dead before we found him, dead before we knew anything was wrong.

The second intruder falls in a cloud of blood, only half visible through the ghost's spectral form.

And then she turns toward us. Jase freezes, his hands still on Lee's chest. He's doing compressions, useless, trying to save something that's already gone. But she doesn't notice nor care. She floats closer, the fury abating, her form getting more detailed as she nears us. She floats over the body of the bigger intruder as if it's nothing.

The headless ghost kneels before the three of us. I'm achingly sad and cold, the feelings breaking through the adrenaline and the fear and the numbness, because we're going to survive this. Jase and I are going to walk out of these woods.

The ghost puts her hand on Lee's chest. I wish she could bring him back from whatever world he's gone to, that she could swipe a hand over his ruined head and the sticky clotting blood and make him whole again. But if she could not save herself, how could I expect her to save him?

I want to cry, like Jase, sobs racking his body as we watch the snow catch in Lee's eyelashes. I want to feel anything other than this awful, aching emptiness.

"You saved us," I say. Not all three—but how could I ask for more?

Her shoulders shift, and again, I get the impression that if she had a head, she'd be looking straight at me. I suddenly have memories that aren't mine: memories of fear and running, of a rough hand catching my shoulder, of the knife sinking into my own throat, as everything fades into a pinprick of light. Memories of dying.

There will be a life after this for me, a time that I move on and this evening in the snow fades into memory. But not for her. She's constantly living her death, constantly caught in the throes of panic, the realization that she is not coming back. I'm momentarily distracted, but brought back by the icy cold on my hand. It's the ghost's hand over mine.

Remember, a voice echoes in my head.

When I look for her again, she's gone. The fog whispers away on the wind.

And I will remember. The blood in the snow and the jagged glass across my front porch, the weight of Lee's body as I hold him against me, the thick smell of copper and shit and ice. The way I wish someone saved her like she saved us.

I'll never be able to forget it.

One-Lane Bridge

by Hannah Whitten

THERE WAS NOTHING TO DO IN RIVERBEND ON A SUMMER NIGHT but steal beers from the minifridge Chase's dad kept in the garage and drink them in the farthest corner of the backyard, so that's what they did.

Mosquitos swarmed up in lacy clouds from the grass, illuminated in the slow-falling light, enticed by the prospect of sweaty skin in chaffing jean shorts. One landed on Jules's thigh, right over the fading swirl of an airbrush tattoo she'd gotten on vacation two weeks ago. She didn't bat it away. She watched it sink its long proboscis into her white leg, watched it drink. She thought of the texts she'd seen to Jenny Horne on Simon's phone this afternoon.

Your so hot.

Trust Simon to cheat on her using the wrong *you're*. It'd be hilarious if it didn't make her entire chest feel like it was being crushed beneath a soccer cleat. The indignity of her long-term boyfriend cheating with the girl who'd told Jules she was too chubby for cheerleading in seventh grade and outed her to the team as bi during freshman year could only be compounded by him not bothering to use proper grammar while he did it.

Jules hated beer, but she took a sip anyway.

Next to her, Lanie was on her third. Her parents were heavy drinkers, and she'd been pilfering from their stash since middle school. Jules hoped she'd stop after three. Drinking made her mean.

"This place is boring as hell." Chase poked morosely at the firepit. "I can't wait to get out of here."

"One more year." Despite the three beers, Lanie's words were crisp, her consonants clear and enunciated. They may have been from small-town Tennessee, but as the near-certain valedictorian of their class, she had bigger plans. She'd told Jules once that the valedictorian shouldn't have a hillbilly accent, that Jules should really work on getting rid of hers if she didn't want to be the cashier at the Gas-N-Go forever.

"One more year," Lanie continued, "and then we'll all be out." Her eyes flicked to Jules. "Well, we'll all be out if Jules can figure out basic algebra anytime soon."

Jules hunched into herself, took another pull of her warming beer. "I got a tutor," she mumbled.

When her dad left two years ago, she'd fallen behind on her schoolwork. Picking it back up had been a struggle.

"Oh, good!" Lanie patted her leg with her moon-pale hand, and it was with genuine warmth. That was the tough thing about Lanie: She could weave between peace and poison fluid as a silverfish, and both of them were true. There wasn't a fake bone in her body, but that almost made it worse. "You'll catch up quick. You know I would've tutored you myself, if I had the time."

Jules could think of very few things she wanted less than to be tutored by Lanie. She, Lanie, Chase, and Simon had been friends since preschool, brought together through close proximity and limited choice, but that mostly just meant they were very aware of the others' weaknesses. Teaching was Lanie's.

"That's great and all, but it doesn't give us anything to do now." Simon leaned back on the grass on Jules's other side, far away enough that they didn't touch. Good. If he tried, she might slap him.

His phone buzzed. Facedown, lighting up the ground around it in a false blue glow, the shadows of weeds and grass blades and creeping ticks waiting for a vein. He eyed the phone, but didn't pick it up.

"What do you suggest, Simon?" Jules smiled, all teeth. "You're good at finding things to do. Especially things you shouldn't be doing."

He glanced at her, brow furrowed beneath the sweep of his light brown hair. There was patchy stubble on his pale, freckled chin. God, Jenny had probably told him he could pull off a beard.

"I dunno." He shrugged, looked away from her. "Going to the movies could be cool, I guess."

Even the way he said *cool* rankled her nerves. She should've said something on the way over. Broken up with him then, the two of them enclosed in the stuffy dark of his pickup, Top 40 on the radio and lukewarm air wheezing through clip-on air fresheners. Jules didn't know why she hadn't. Maybe because it was their last summer, maybe because as much as this nightly ritual in Chase's backyard was stifling, it was at least familiar. They'd clung to each other this long because it was comfortable, like ivy guided up a fence, and she didn't have the energy to break that. Not yet.

Because if she and Simon broke up, all four of them would. Something this brittle couldn't survive that kind of cracking.

"You know what we should do?" There was a glassy light in Chase's eyes as he downed the rest of his beer. His pale hands flashed in the dusk, like fireflies. "We should go to the Bridge."

The pitiful fire spat smoke. The buzzing harmony of night-bugs burrowed into their ears.

"Sure." Jules jammed her half-full bottle into a grass tussock. It tipped over anyway, spilled foam. "Why the hell not."

Lanie frowned, already shaking her head. "No. That's a stupid idea. Your ideas are always stupid, Chase."

Chase waved a middle finger in her direction. "Got any better ones, *salutatorian?*"

Lanie's hand curled around her beer bottle, chipped purple nail polish clicking against green glass. "It's tied," she hissed. "We have all of senior year."

"Whatever. If my ideas are so stupid, let's see you use your huge brain to come up with something better to do than go to the Bridge." Chase waggled his eyebrows. "Don't be scared of the Bridge, Lanie-Loo. It's summer—nothing bad happens in summer."

"Have you *ever* watched a horror movie?"

"Whitmer Way is only like a mile from here; we can get there in five minutes," Jules said. Next to her, Simon's phone vibrated again. She didn't look at it, and neither did he. "I mean, we're way too busy to do this kind of shit during the school year. This might be our only chance to find out if the stories are true."

"They aren't true," Lanie said, but it was faint.

The Bridge had a name. Or Jules assumed it had, at one point. It was part of Whitmer Way, the back-road shortcut winding over the mountain between Riverbend and Gwensville that you took when you wanted to avoid highway traffic or highway cops. Now everyone just called it the Bridge, and it had become a convenient folklore scapegoat for the high amount of disappearances in the area.

The legend was that the Bridge belonged to something inhuman, some creature lurking in the surrounding woods that had been there long before the town was. An elemental, tied to the land, a being made of fear and forest. Jules thought that sounded too wishy-washy, a purposefully vague explanation for the missing hikers and runaways—easier to accept than the thought that humans sometimes did terrible things to each other, that fleeing into the woods might be a better alternative than living in the homes of some of your neighbors. No one wanted to think that a person you passed in the Piggly Wiggly might be a monster.

But anyone who'd been to the Bridge could feel that there was . . . *something* out there. Something that made your skin rise in goose bumps and your hair spike along the back of your neck. Something that plucked at all the bad feelings in your chest— your anger, your fear, your selfishness—and drew them out, played them like a violin.

Jules was full of those feelings tonight. So full, she could burst.

"Fine, so we go to the damn Bridge." Lanie pulled another beer from the cooler, popped the top with practiced ease. "What exactly do we do there? Just wait around and see if something spooky happens? That's basically what we're doing now."

"We gotta do something to make it happen, I think," Jules said. Other than watching the *Charmed* remake, she didn't have much experience with anything witchy, but surely it wouldn't be hard. "Something to . . . activate it, or whatever." She shrugged. "We could bleed on it, I guess. That seems ritual-y."

"Oh *hell* yeah." Chase reached up to push back his blond hair; he'd had more than his fair share from the cooler, and his hand went a little south of his forehead. "We should go bleed on the Bridge and light a candle at midnight. Maybe we'll get a crossroads demon. Make deals to get into good colleges."

"More likely we'll get tetanus." But Lanie was into it now; she leaned forward, legs crossed, undoubtedly thinking about how she could spin this into one of her college essays. "Plus, isn't the Bridge supposed to belong to some kind of woods ghosty thing, not a crossroads demon? Those are entirely different entities."

"Lanie coming in clutch with the cryptid classifications," Jules said. Lanie swatted her leg.

"Come on, seriously." Chase's eyes were bright as he leaned in toward the fire. "Tucker and Chris went last year, but they chickened out and left before it got dark. So if we go now, we're already ahead of them."

"Is this really about getting back at the guy who stole your boyfriend?" Lanie rolled her eyes.

Chase just gave her the bird again.

"I dunno." The two words seemed to be the majority of Simon's vocabulary tonight, and it made Jules want to scream.

The bonfire light on Chase's face twisted the angles, made them strange. "You scared, dude?"

"Yeah, Simon. You scared?" Jules turned to look him in the

eye for the first time that night.

He couldn't hold her gaze for long. His eyes slipped away, back to their pathetic fire. He finally picked up his phone, looked at the screen. Put it back, facedown.

Something rose in Jules's chest, something burning and thorny, like she'd swallowed poison ivy and it'd taken root. She wanted the Bridge with a sudden fierceness, wanted the graffiti-strewn boards beneath her feet and the rusty railings at her side, wanted to scream into the woods and see what screamed back.

It's all that anger, her therapist had told her, in that white-painted office with a slippery leather couch and expensive paperweights on the bookshelf. *You have so much anger, Jules, and you need to find constructive ways to express it.*

Going to a possibly haunted bridge probably wasn't what Dr. Pollard had in mind, but beggars and choosers and all that shit.

"The monster is a joke," Jules spat, with enough venom that Lanie shot her a questioning sidelong look. "Like, come on, it's not even a good story. Y'all are really scared of a monster without a *plotline?*"

They all stared at each other, glassy-eyed and halfway to a fight. It hung around their heads like cigarette smoke, close and cloying and not entirely understood.

Then Simon pushed up from the grass, bringing his phone with him, slipping it into his pocket. "Let's go then, bitches."

They took Chase's car, a battered Honda Pilot that smelled like weed and Axe body spray. Lanie went inside the house as the rest of them claimed seats, and came back out with a candle—cheap and pine-scented, Walmart brand.

The stereo pounded through some heavy metal mix that Chase used for football workouts as they drove up the winding road to the Bridge. The houses on Whitmer Way were the kind that could've been nice—deep porches and stone chimneys, dormer windows. But the residents didn't care about having cute houses, so the siding peeled under the dormer windows, trash littered the deep porches, and the yards were choked with defunct appliances and old cars on blocks. Too-skinny dogs barked at them as they passed, baying drowned out by bass.

They didn't talk, not really, other than Simon telling Chase a song sucked, and Lanie complaining that the air conditioner never worked and they should've taken her car instead. Trivial things, words fed into the rush of summer wind through open windows. Stays against silence.

Jules, hand lolling out the window, tried to remember the last time they'd really talked, had a conversation that scraped below surface level. She couldn't.

It didn't take long to reach the Bridge. Chase turned down the music, stopped the car. It cut out right in the middle of a guitar riff, and the squeal of it echoed in the dark trees, an unresolved chord that made Jules's neck itch.

"Five minutes to midnight," Chase said quietly.

Jules opened her door. The thorny heat in her chest still lived there, sharp and brambled, and she slammed the door closed harder than she had to. "Let's move, then."

The Bridge itself didn't look like anything special. Rough wooden boards bracketing a strip of gray asphalt. Rusty metal rails. Below, a creek bed, the water long gone in the deep dry of a Tennessee summer, leaving only mud and underbrush.

Graffiti covered the entire structure, layers of it from years of bored teenagers. Pentagrams and sloppy crosses, names and birthdays and phone numbers. Simon toed at a smiley face with Xs over the eyes. "We should've brought some spray paint."

"You didn't even want to come, and now you want to tag it?" Jules gave him a withering look. "Make up your mind, Simon."

"What is your *problem*?" He whirled around, genuine hurt on his face, and wasn't that funny, wasn't it just fucking hilarious, that *she* was hurting *his* feelings while his phone lit up in his pocket again?

Jules stepped up until they were closer than they'd been all night. She smiled. "You left your phone at my house today," she said carefully, sweetly. "When you left to go grab lunch."

She hadn't meant to snoop. She wasn't that kind of person. But when she'd seen Jenny's name strobe across the cracked screen, curiosity got the better of her. Jules should've said something then, the minute Simon walked in the door with his arms full of Taco Bell—but silence had gripped her, cold hands of indecision around her throat. Now the silence let her go and the decision was made, but she still didn't say anything outright, didn't name the thing and make it a weapon.

Because this moment—teasing him with her knowledge without telling him the whole, leaving him dangling as realization spread over his face, florid as a sunrise when you stay up all night—god, this felt good. It fed the burn of her anger, kindling for its fire.

Maybe that's why she'd kept the silence, cupped it close to her chest like a broken-winged bird. Waiting for this, waiting for the Bridge. Waiting for the look on Simon's face and the beginning of that long, spiderwebbing crack down their brittle center.

"So," Jules said, "you tell me what my problem is, Simon. Because I think you know."

Simon just stared at her. He looked almost scared.

Good.

"Y'all coming or what?" Chase and Lanie were already on the Bridge, too far away to overhear. Lanie was trying to light the candle with her Zippo; she kept burning the tip of her thumb. Finally, the wick caught, spinning fake-pine-needle scent into the air.

"Yep." Jules edged around Simon, making sure no part of her

touched him. After a moment, he followed.

Chase brandished something in the air as they approached. A safety pin. "Found this behind the visor. We can use it to prick our fingers."

Lanie's nose wrinkled. "I hope you all got your shots. And everyone's been tested recently?"

Affirmative grunts, distracted, all of them looking at the surrounding woods instead of each other. The air felt close and thick, and the pines seemed to almost bow toward them, like when a kid hid behind a curtain. Jules felt like she was being watched. The moon was a stage light and they were taking their places, following an expected script.

Too much beer. Beer and adrenaline and all that *anger*.

Lanie went first, poking the pin at the pad of her thumb until a bead of blood surfaced. She frowned at it a moment, then wiped it on the rusty railing. "Let me get valedictorian," she muttered.

Jules snorted. "So we're making wishes on it now?"

A self-conscious shrug as Lanie plucked a tiny bottle of vodka from her back pocket and poured a thin stream over the pin. "Seemed appropriate." She wagged the bottle at Chase. "You know how stupid it is to keep this in your glove box, right?"

"Like the cops around here give a damn as long as the football team keeps winning." Chase took the pin and jabbed it at his finger, then wiped the blood next to Lanie's before pouring vodka over the metal. "Let me get into a better college than Tucker.

Better yet, make Tucker just not get into college at all."

Simon went next. He slid an unreadable look to Jules as the pin brought blood. "Help everyone to stay cool," he muttered. "And not get madder than they should over things that aren't big deals."

She could've pitched him over the side of the Bridge, into the muddy creek bed below. It was a miracle she didn't, really. Those bowing pines and the heavy air seemed to be waiting for it.

Jules grabbed the pin, shoved it into her thumb. Too far—it stung, the residual vodka making it burn enough to drive her teeth together. Blood welled; she held up her thumb toward the sky like a beacon. "Let everyone get what they deserve. But especially Simon."

Simon narrowed his eyes. "You need to chill, Jules."

And this wasn't the time for her silence to finally snap, wasn't the place to do something like this, but rage bubbled too far up her throat to not let it escape out her mouth. The atmosphere here—the oppressive heat, the electric spark of the air, the heavy regard of tall pines and warm dirt and the feeling of being *observed*, somehow—seemed to take her anger and magnify it, like an angled glass on an ant. And she let it.

"Do I?" Jules snapped, pointing at Simon with her bloody finger. "Or maybe *you* need to—"

"Cut it out," Chase interrupted, eyes skittering nervously back and forth over the dark trees. "If you're gonna blow up, the

Bridge is not the best place for it."

"Seems like the perfect place for it, actually." Jules felt her face twist, her teeth bared in the candle's smoky glow, and Simon actually backed away when she took a step toward him. "Do you know how *cowardly* you are? You've always been spineless, Simon, but this one really takes the cake."

The atmosphere around her seemed to be . . . bright, almost, as she ripped into Simon. Like some slow, building light gradually filled the space behind her. But Jules only half noticed, too focused on Simon's stricken face, relishing the look of pain that flashed across it.

"Hey," Chase said, holding up a hand, his eyes trained beyond her. "Jules—"

"Cowardly and spineless and *groveling*," she continued, spitting the words, ignoring Chase. "All you had to do was break up with me first. Is that so hard? But no, you're so conflict-avoidant, you'd rather text Jenny fucking Horne behind my back. Is that really the best you could do—"

"Jules!"

Angry girl.

Lanie's voice had spoken her name, but there was another voice beneath it. A quiet one, a reverberating one that sounded like layers of leaves and a mouth full of grave dirt. It was enough to shut Jules up, make her whip around to face the trees.

The forest seemed to sigh.

Then—light. Blinding, breaking through the pines, growing steadily brighter until it nearly eclipsed them. Jules stumbled back, hand held to her chest, blood dripping down her arm instead of rubbed on the railing with the others.

"Car," Chase called, though the glow was far too intense for headlights. "Clear out!"

They ran toward the Pilot, Simon and Chase and Lanie, but Jules stayed on the Bridge, her blood winding a slow red river toward her elbow. The light hurt her eyes, but she looked straight into it, until all she saw was white.

"Jules!" A hand on her arm. "Move your ass!"

She let Lanie pull her into Chase's car. He started it up, the heavy guitar riff finally resolving the chord, and did a tight U-turn that almost landed them in scrub bushes before heading back toward his house.

Adrenaline mended a multitude of cracks, at least on the surface; they were laughing now, talking excitedly, sticking sore thumbs in their mouths. "Shit," Lanie hissed, "we left the candle and the vodka!"

Jules wiped her bloody arm on her T-shirt. She said nothing. For a brief moment, back there on the Bridge, she'd felt . . . free. The burden of her anger lifted, the burn in her middle assuaged. But now it was back, and she felt its weight all the more for the temporary reprieve.

Chase pulled into his driveway, switched off the music; the

clock said 1:00 a.m. "Curfew," Simon groaned, opening the passenger-side door. He turned to Jules, guarded. "We gotta go."

"Lanie can take me."

Quiet, but for the cicadas.

"I mean," Lanie said slowly, "I guess I can, but—"

"I'm done." Jules said it slowly, enunciating each syllable. She didn't look at Simon; she looked instead at the trail of rust on her pale skin, tracking between freckles like the lines drawn to make constellations. "I'm done with you, Simon. This is over. You and Jenny have fun."

Then she got out of the car. She walked over to Lanie's Corolla, opened the door, slipped inside. If the others talked, she didn't listen. She leaned her head back and closed her eyes and waited for Lanie to come drive her home.

She did. They were silent the whole time. When Jules got out at the house she shared with her mom, the same house her dad used to live in before he ran off with his secretary, she didn't say goodbye.

And none of them talked for two months.

"Hey."

Jules cradled her phone between her chin and her shoulder, fishing her keys out of her pocket and shoving them into the front door. Mom wouldn't be home for at least two hours; she'd left out meat to brown in the skillet.

And Lanie was on the phone.

"Hey." Lanie's voice sounded normal, but there was a timidity lurking behind it, one you wouldn't hear unless you knew her as well as Jules did. "Uh, how are things?"

"Fine." And they were. Yeah, she and Lanie and Simon and Chase hadn't talked since that night in the summer, but they all got busy once school started, and all told, them falling out of contact wasn't that strange. They were glued together in ways that months of not talking didn't dissolve, for better or worse.

Usually worse, Jules thought.

"Good, good." A pause. Jules could almost picture Lanie pacing back and forth in front of the big window seat in her room, the one they'd sat on to read the entire Warrior Cats series the summer they were ten. "Listen, would you want to go to the football game on Friday? With me and Simon and Chase?"

Jules dropped her backpack right inside the door. She gnawed on her bottom lip.

"I know it might be weird with you and Simon," Lanie continued, following a script she'd no doubt rehearsed for this phone call, "but at least he and Jenny aren't hooking up anymore."

Surprise, surprise. She'd never expected *that* to last long.

"It's just . . . I miss us, you know?" Lanie sighed down the phone. "And I know it won't ever be how it was—I know it can't ever be like that again—but I want us to be together. One last time."

And maybe it was because it was Tuesday and she'd aced her algebra pop quiz, or because she knew they were going to have tacos for dinner, or because she'd finished all her homework and could binge bad vampire shows all night. Or maybe it was because she missed them all being together too. Either way, Jules found herself nodding. Found herself saying yes. Found herself thinking maybe it would be different, maybe it'd changed, maybe they really could be good together, all four of them.

Unlikely, but she could hope. The same way she always did.

They made plans for Lanie to come by early on Friday so they could drive to Gwensville for coffee before the game. And when Jules hung up, she was actually, genuinely excited.

Excited enough that when she remembered how Lanie phrased it—*one last time*—she shrugged it off as momentary weirdness. Nothing to think too hard about.

She went to brown the ground beef before Mom got home.

"You'll be glad you have it for the game, I promise. It'll keep your hands warm." Lanie took a sip of her latte as she pulled back onto the road from the Gwensville Starbucks. It was the only one in the county, and thus, they'd waited in line for at least half an hour.

"It'll be gone before we get there, and it's seventy-five degrees outside." Jules had opted for hot chocolate, and it was so rich, she had to take ridiculously tiny sips. "Between your boots and your cardigan, you'll be sweating before second base."

"Oh my *god*, it's football. There are no bases."

"Whatever. Before the second . . . football equivalent of base."

Lanie arched an auburn brow, close to being actually annoyed. "You're hopeless."

Jules grinned around the rim of her cup. This was . . . nice. She and Lanie had fallen right back into old patterns, like no time had passed at all. And it was nice, it was familiar, it was glue on the fissures of something slowly breaking.

She'd take it.

"We're gonna miss kickoff." Lanie's mascaraed eyes kept flickering from the clock on the dashboard to the rapidly darkening twilight surrounding Gwensville's main drag. She seemed nervous, fingers twisting around her paper cup, knee jittering back and forth as her foot pressed the gas. It made the leather of her boot squeak against her heel.

"Does that matter?" Jules asked, in a tone that made it clear it didn't matter to *her*.

"I mean, kind of." Lanie shrugged, took a drink, eyes fixed on the road ahead and the rapidly darkening sky. "That's when I told Chase and Simon we'd meet them. They'll be waiting. And Chase won't want to miss seeing the whole thing, since he's benched for his ankle for at least two more games." She took in a deep breath.

"We could take Whitmer Way, I guess."

The name of the road made Jules's lips press together. Made something that felt like thorns and poison bloom prickly heat in her chest. "Seriously?"

Lanie shrugged, stilted and mechanical. "It's a shortcut." Her eyes stared straight ahead, watching the road disappear beneath the cab. "Might as well."

Jules gnawed the balm off her bottom lip. If they were really going to take Whitmer Way, they had to decide fast—the exit was on the left, scattered rocks from the road's end already catching the headlights, throwing tiny shadows.

"What the hell," she muttered. "Sure. Let's do it."

Lanie let out a long breath, almost like she'd been holding it. Then she swung the wheel.

The tires crunched from asphalt to gravel, making them both lurch in their seats. Jules clutched her hot chocolate.

Derelict houses loomed on either side of the road, angles twisted to monstrous by the falling light. The leaves were still thick on the trees, not yet succumbing to the slow encroachment of autumn, and it made the darkness heavy, almost viscous.

"I hate this road," Lanie murmured under her breath, knuckles white on the wheel. "God, I hate this."

"Chill out." Jules turned down the music on instinct, as if they were crawling through enemy territory. "This was *your* idea, and it's not like you haven't been out here before."

Exactly the wrong thing to say. Lanie stiffened. "Can we not talk about that?"

Fear in her voice, which unsettled Jules far more than the expected irritation would have. "Yeah," she said, shifting in her seat. "Yeah, sorry."

God. They were ruining it, again. Finding those cracks and poking at them.

Lanie nodded, one jerk of her chin. They lapsed once more into uneasy silence.

The sky darkened further, the trees a shadowed blur striated in the headlights. Lanie sat still and quiet in the driver's seat, hands at ten and two. Her coffee had to be cold by now. Jules's hot chocolate was. She wanted to roll down the window and pour it out, but the idea of breaking the barrier between the inside of the car and the woods made her skin crawl.

Jules sighed, slumping against the window. "It wasn't like it was scary," she said quietly. Even as she spoke, she knew she should opt for silence, but the thorny thing in her chest wouldn't let her. The thorny thing in her chest seemed to grow the farther they drove, the closer they got to that stupid Bridge, as if it were drawing all her anger out, making it snap beneath her breastbone. "Nothing happened. We were there for ten minutes before—"

"Shut *up*, Jules."

Her teeth clicked together.

Lanie shook her head, slowly. "You don't get it," she

murmured. "Okay? You just don't get it."

"Don't get what? That we did something stupid two months ago and now we're going to drive over the site where said stupid thing occurred? What is there to *get?*"

Lanie's lips pressed together.

The anger in Jules's chest flared hotter, brighter. "Maybe you're right." That barbed voice again, the same one she'd used on Simon the night of the blood and the candle and the Bridge, sugar-sweet and sharper for it. "Maybe it *was* scary if you were drunk. You should really watch it, Lanie. Don't want to end up like dear old dad."

More silence, but she saw Lanie's hands twitch around the steering wheel. "You know, you can be a real bitch sometimes," she said softly, almost inflectionless. "I shouldn't feel sorry for you."

"No, Lanie, you definitely should not." Jules snorted, shook her head. "Actually, scratch that, because I feel bad for *all* of us. I feel bad that we keep pretending like we're friends when we're clearly not anymore, when all we ever do is . . . is *claw* at each other. Maybe it was friendship once, when we were little kids, but it sure as shit isn't anymore. And we've all been stupid to keep pretending. People grow apart, it's natural, but when you try to trap them into the same place they've always been, things go rotten."

That's what had happened. They'd stagnated, gone rotten. They were so afraid of change, so afraid of becoming new people, they'd shackled each other to the corpses of who they'd been before.

"So you don't think we're all friends anymore?" Lanie whispered to the road.

"No." Jules took a deep breath. "No, I don't."

Some of the nervousness seemed to ease out of Lanie's shoulders, like something she'd dreaded had been taken care of. "Hmm," she said.

Jules's mouth tasted like bile; her throat felt like she'd swallowed a cheese grater. She curled against the door, as far away from Lanie as she could get, and closed her eyes. Once they got to the game, she'd find another friend, bum a ride home. There was nothing here to fix anymore. The brittle thing had finally shattered.

A car pulled out in front of them, a wild swing of headlights. Lanie wrenched the wheel, sending the nose of the Corolla closer to the trees than the road.

Jules straightened. "What the hell was that?"

Lanie rubbed at her throat, where the seat belt had dug in. She didn't answer.

The car that had pulled out in front of them shot down the road, a blur of black metal against the dark pines. Jules squinted after it like she could make out the license plate, but it was gone too quickly, disappearing around another curve.

Foot still on the brake, Lanie reached for her phone, tapped out a quick message. The blue screen bathed them in ghostlight, made it seem even darker when she pressed the lock button and eased the car onto the road again. All in silence, all with her face toward the road, completely ignoring Jules.

"Whatever," Jules muttered under her breath, and she wasn't sure if she meant it for Lanie or the car or this whole damn night.

The Bridge was up ahead, five minutes of driving, tops. It seemed Lanie was determined to spend those minutes in silence, and Jules was no longer in the mood to try to change that.

The pines slipped by. Fog slithered at the edges of the road, cut through by the headlights, weak swaths of yellow glow. Jules shifted in her seat, tried to calm the nonsensical way her pulse climbed higher into her throat, beating at her wrists like the bass drum in a marching band. It was fear, but it was also . . . exhilaration. A feeling like something finally slotting into place, patience rewarded.

Stupid. It was a bridge, that's all (and she thought very hard to de-capitalize it in her brain, to smash down the *B* that made it anything more). A bridge where nothing happened, a bridge that was nothing but bad graffiti and worse urban legends. If there'd been anything to see, they would've seen it that night over the summer, before the cop car scared them off—

It was *a cop, right?*

Had to be. Jules remembered the lights, remembered— but, no, did she actually remember the red and blue streaking the forest around it in asinine patriotic colors? They'd all thought it was a cop, but now that she was trying, she couldn't quite conjure the solid shape of a memory. Lights, yes, but not police lights. Not even headlights, really. Just one light, beaming at them through the trees, eclipsing the forest in a strange and directionless brilliance.

Through the whole drive, Lanie didn't make a sound. And after five minutes of swimming in that silence, the Bridge loomed out of the fog. Her headlights cut over a new bit of graffiti at the very front, sliced over the wood in lurid, dripping red.

Drop for drop.

Lanie slowed when she reached it, though they were barely going thirty as it was. It took a minute for Jules to realize why.

A car was parked on the Bridge's other side.

Dark metal against darker trees, the catch of Lanie's headlights the only illumination. Tinted windows showed nothing of what might be waiting inside. The car was at a dead stop just beyond the opposite lip of the Bridge, blocking the one-lane road, leaving no way to get around it.

Ten miles an hour, then five, the Corolla creeping past the pronouncement of *drop for drop* to come to rest directly in the center of the Bridge. Maybe if they saw them coming, they'd move? The Bridge wasn't necessarily a hookup spot, but Jules guessed there was a first time for everything, and the possibility of being swept up by whatever otherworldly being was supposed to haunt the area might get some people hot and bothered.

But Lanie came to a stop, motor purring, and the car on the

other side of the Bridge didn't move.

Lanie's hands dropped from the steering wheel and into her lap, blanched in the blue light from the dash. Music still murmured from the speakers, an old country song barely a breath above silence. A plucked banjo, mournful.

For a moment, Jules sat there, frozen, not exactly fearful but somewhere close to it. The skin between her shoulder blades prickled, that sense of being somewhere that didn't belong to her. Like pressing against a soap bubble and waiting for it to pop.

And the bristling heat in her chest was still there, heightened to a fever.

Jules reached over Lanie and honked, just slightly, though the sound seemed to echo and reverberate through the pines and the rock and the dry creek bed. She winced and snatched her hand from the wheel, sending them back into silence. Lanie just sat still, didn't try to stop her. Didn't try to do anything.

"What do we do?" She turned to Lanie, the tension and bitchiness of the last hour forgotten. "Like . . . they aren't moving."

"I dunno." Lanie swallowed, shrugged. Her expression was empty and wan, washed an otherworldly blue. "I dunno, Jules."

Her fingers twitched to a fist, mind whiting out to nothing but the desire to drive it into Lanie's stupid blank face. "Seriously?"

Another shrug. Lanie flinched away from her, though Jules hadn't moved in her direction at all. She turned toward the window, away from Jules.

"Fine." Jules unbuckled her seat belt like she was drawing a sword, slammed her cold paper cup into the space between the console and the two older fast-food cups currently occupying the holder. "Fine, Lanie. You sit here and be useless." She tugged at the door handle.

"I'm sorry," Lanie breathed.

And Jules wanted to ask her for what, Jules wanted to make her apologize with some specificity, but she was too angry, and she didn't think Lanie would answer anyway. Sorry for all of it. Sorry that the closeness they'd once had was fractured and shrapnel-shattered now, cracked by years of forced proximity that did nothing but smother. Sorry they were late to the game, sorry they were fighting, sorry they couldn't hold it together for one more year.

"Yeah, me too," Jules said. Then she opened the door and stepped out into the night.

It was cooler than she thought it would be. October first and seventy-five degrees, according to the thermostat in the car, but it felt much chillier here on the mountain, here on the Bridge. She tugged her thin cardigan around herself and fought off a shiver, suddenly stricken with the enormity of what she was doing. There was no way to know who was in that car, or why, or what they would do. Monsters at the Piggly Wiggly.

But she wasn't just going to *stand* here.

"Hey!" She meant to yell, but it came out at a conversational volume, her vocal cords unwilling to shatter the dark silence any more than they had to.

Nothing. The car was still. The trees were still. The stars above the tops of the pines were pinpricks in the dark, needles through a black curtain that billowed toward her slowly, so slowly.

"Hey, assholes, you're blocking the road." Again, conversational, timid. Why could she only summon poison when it was to hurt people she'd once cared about?

One heartbeat. Another.

Then the doors of the car opened.

Jules stumbled back, one hand up like she could defend herself with it. Too late, she thought of the pepper spray in her bag, a birthday gift from her father she'd rolled her eyes at, mailed straight to her from Amazon with no note on the receipt. She lurched toward Lanie's passenger side, wondering if she'd have time to grab it, if they were armed—

"Jules."

Simon.

Slowly, she turned, still clutching her cardigan like a lifeline. Simon stood at the side of the black car on the other end of the Bridge, a vague shape in the dark, but one she'd know anywhere. His hair was recently cut, leached colorless in the starlight. His jacket hung on him like a scarecrow. She'd have thought it ridiculous an hour ago, but in the unnatural chill, it seemed practical.

He stood still, staring. It occurred to Jules that the way he'd said her name didn't sound surprised.

She stopped her fearful crawl toward her bag and the pepper spray, brow furrowed. "What are you doing here?" Then, though it seemed like a stupid thing to say: "Aren't we meeting you at the football game?"

Simon didn't say anything. The driver's-side door of the dark car opened, Chase climbing out with the slightest limp from his twisted ankle. It shouldn't have been a surprise, but Jules's stomach still lurched.

Behind her, another car door shutting, a click that seemed to echo. "No, Jules," Lanie said quietly, her white skin cast red in the gleam of the taillights. "We aren't meeting them at the football game."

A moment, stretched, to take all of it in, to understand the un-understandable. Dark night, lonesome bridge, empty road, and the three people she'd been closest to in the world. Closeness that had rotted, stagnated, curdled.

Jules backed up, hand shooting out of its own accord, clawing at the railing like it could hold her up. Her friends—that wasn't the right word, she'd just told Lanie that wasn't the right word, but god, it was hard to think of another—just watched her go, none of them moving to stop her, and that was more terrifying than if they'd launched forward with their teeth bared.

"It's no use running." Chase's voice usually sounded joke-ready, bright and brassy. Now it was tired, like his throat was a dishrag someone had wrung out. "We tried. It wants your sins, Jules, and you can't run from those."

"But it's different for *her*." This from Lanie, tack-sharp and grating. "*She* didn't give her sacrifice to the Bridge. It's not in her fucking *head*."

"Wasn't her fault." Simon's hair hung lank over his forehead, blue eyes wan. "We were interrupted before we got to her."

"Because you just had to pop off at Simon *right then*, Jules." Lanie spat her name. "You couldn't just *wait*, and it got in our heads, made us see——" Her voice broke; she pressed the back of her wrist against her teeth. A deep breath, then she turned to Jules, eyes shining flat and tear-gilded. "The monster is real, Jules. The one you thought was such a joke that night."

Her brain was crime tape and scrolling text below TV footage. *Local teens go bananas, kill friend on the Bridge.* The paper would probably use the place's real name, but Jules could not for the life of her remember it.

"The monster is real," Lanie repeated, her pretty brown eyes wide and glassy and fixed on Jules, "and it wants you."

Jules's shaking fingers knocked against something on the railing, something with give—the stump of the green candle, now completely devoid of fake pine scent. Her nails scraped across it, collecting verdant wax beneath them. The candle toppled off the rail, landed in the creek bed below with a strangely meaty *thunk*.

It slammed her back from some kind of stasis, forced herself into her body. Jules turned and ran.

No use running, Chase had said. But instinct was impossible to fight, and her feet churned gravel, sending her careening around the bridge, into the trees. Her boot landed on the new graffiti. *Drop for drop.*

She'd pricked her finger, but she'd never given her blood to the Bridge. To whatever lived on the Bridge. Whatever had pulled out her anger, churned it up her throat like a table-rapper's ectoplasm, wanted to *own* it. Own her.

Because that's what would happen. She knew it in a lightning streak of thought. If Lanie and the others got her—killed her, that's what they wanted, and she knew that too—then she'd belong to the Bridge.

A crooked step; her ankle turned. Jules screamed, unearthly in the dark woods, knees hitting the ground a moment before her palms did. White-hot pain flared up her calf, but she barely had time to register it before the dirt beneath her gave way. With another hoarse cry, Jules slipped down the steep embankment, body forced into a roll. The razor edges of ferns whipped her face; her wrist smacked against a tree trunk. She felt the delicate bones crunch beneath her skin.

When Jules finally came to a stop, she was on her stomach in the middle of the creek bed, the Bridge a black shadow cutting the starlight above. The pines whispered, whispered.

Angry girl, they said.

She groaned. Tried to sit up. Couldn't. Her body felt like one big bruise, and her wrist was definitely broken—she looked at it, once, and the angle was all wrong, twisted enough to make her guts knot up. But her ankle seemed okay. Okay enough to walk, anyway.

Jules set her teeth and pushed with her unbroken wrist. Slowly, her body levered up from the ground, mud clinging to her clothes, packing the scrapes that ran down her face, her arms. Jules panted at the ground, gathering the strength to stand.

But a foot planted itself in between her shoulder blades. "Not so fast, Juju."

Juju. A nickname from elementary school, one that only ever caught on with Lanie. She'd stopped using it this year, long before summer, long before the Bridge. Why hadn't Jules noticed that?

She tried to flip over, to wiggle out from beneath Lanie's boot, but the pain in her wrist and her ankle was too much, and the mud sucking at her limbs made it nearly impossible.

"It's pointless." Lanie sounded sorry, at least. The anger that had laced her voice up on the Bridge had cooled into sorrowing resignation. "I loved you, Juju. You know I did, and I still do, if I'm honest. Even if none of us are good for each other anymore."

And wasn't that the worst part, every time? How the love and the caring stayed, even as everything around it rotted?

"But we can't let you go," Lanie said. "The Bridge gets what it wants. *It* gets what it wants."

"I don't understand." A bare breath of sound, pluming from Jules's mouth like smoke. "Lanie, I don't understand."

Lanie's boots crunched in the rock and dirt as she crouched next to her. Cool fingers pushed Jules's sweaty hair off her forehead. "Whatever we did that night, with the candle and the blood . . . it worked." She swallowed, cast a nervous glance over her shoulder at the whispering trees. "It summoned the . . . the thing that lives here, the thing that owns the Bridge. But we were wrong. It doesn't grant wishes, doesn't make bargains. It's just interested in human weakness. The sin that runs the deepest in a person. It tastes it through your blood."

A safety pin and a Walmart candle, beer-silly and scared. Apparently, it was no sophisticated business, summoning devils.

"It got a taste of all of us," Lanie continued. "Except you. But it didn't need your blood on the Bridge to know how angry you were, Jules. It could tongue it out of the *air*." The look in her eyes as they cut over to Jules was shocked, even though Lanie was the one contemplating murder. "And it decided it wanted you, *all* of you. Wanted you enough to get in our heads and make us bring you back."

Carefully, Jules tensed her muscles, seeing if they'd move. They mostly did, though her wrist felt like a bag of broken glass, and her ankle twinged so hard, she had to bite down a scream. "Then we'll try to make it stop," she said, though it was more to keep Lanie talking than for any hope she would listen. "I'll help you."

"This *is* how you help, Jules. It wants your blood, so we'll give it to the Bridge." Lanie's mouth drew into a tight line. "If we don't give it yours, it will take our families'."

Jules's breath whistled in and out of her mouth. Pain made her head feel both light and heavy at the same time. Still, she curled her toes under, tried to work free of the mud.

"The dreams were awful, after that night." Now that she'd started talking, it seemed like Lanie couldn't stop. "And vivid. Some mornings I woke up thinking I'd actually done it. That I'd taken the axe . . ." She trailed off, swallowed. "I would have, if it kept on for much longer. I know it. So would Simon and Chase— Chase twisted his own fucking *ankle* to make sure he couldn't get up in the middle of the night. It would've made us kill our whole families if we didn't bring you to it."

"But the light . . ." Jules's mouth tasted like blood; she turned her head to the side and spat. "It wasn't a cop. It was . . . whatever lives here. If it wanted my blood, why interrupt us?"

"It didn't. It was on the way. When you ripped into Simon, we paused the ritual, then we saw the light and left. *You* interrupted *it*." She straightened, standing over Jules like an avenging angel. "We saved you when we left. I wouldn't have, if I'd known. I would've let it take you then."

Jules twitched on the ground. All that rage, simmering to a boil in her chest for so long, had cooled to smooth, gleaming dread.

"It's you, or them." Lanie took a deep breath. Something

shining emerged from next to her leg. A pocketknife. "And I'm sorry, Juju, but this is easier to live with."

The knife rose, a shimmering line in the dark. Jules closed her eyes, prepared to lurch upward.

But the blade never came. A cry, a rush of air, and when Jules opened her eyes, Simon stood over her, chest heaving, the knife clutched in his hand. He looked at it, then threw it into the brush.

"What did you do?" It still came out accusing, even now when he'd just saved her life.

"She's fine." Simon gestured to the side—Lanie lay in a heap, a bruise blooming on her temple. "Or, she will be."

"No, she won't." Jules forced herself to roll over, even though the motion made all her nerve endings scream. "None of you will be, isn't that the whole point? The thing—"

"There has to be another way." Simon's voice was hoarse; he rubbed his hand over his forehead, smearing dirt. "I can't live with being a murderer, Jules. Not with my family, not with you. I know things ended badly; I know we don't even like each other anymore. But I can't kill you." He heaved a shaky sigh. "We aren't friends. But we *were*."

"Well," Jules said to the sky. "That's something."

Simon offered her a hand. She took it, reaching awkwardly since he stood on the side with her broken wrist, and let him haul her up, throw an arm around his shoulder. Already, the unreality of the past twenty minutes was fading away, her brain whiting out information that made no logical sense, painting it dream-like. Maybe it *was* a dream. Maybe tomorrow, when she looked at all of it in the cold autumn light, it would be ridiculous.

They all needed help if they believed what Lanie had told her. About the monster, about the dreams, killing their families. Jules would have to call someone, do something. But that could be tomorrow. Tonight she could—

The light didn't bloom gradually this time. It burst like a dying star, flooding the trees, the creek bed, the Bridge itself, blinding-bright. Next to her, Simon cried out, dropped away. Jules fell to her knees.

In the light ahead of her, a dark shape moved slowly forward.

The thing that owned the Bridge. The thing that wanted her.

Jules didn't back away. Didn't falter. All the anger within her that had drawn this monster out in the first place flared to flaming life. But there was a difference to it. The edges had softened, made it something she could grasp without cutting her hands.

Dr. Pollard said she had a hard time expressing her anger because she had a hard time *owning* it. It felt like something outside herself, something that happened to her. And Jules had tried and tried to integrate it, to understand it as part of her rather than an invader, and she'd never quite managed it.

Until now. Until something that wanted to take it from her strode forward in brilliant, awful light, a slow eclipse that would end in her ending.

If she let it.

"How dare you," she snarled.

The vague shape stopped. What looked like its head cocked to the side.

"How *dare* you," she said again, stronger this time, clear and ringing. "None of this is for you. *Nothing* I feel is yours to take. You got a taste, and that's all you're getting. Do you understand?"

The figure didn't move. Didn't speak.

"I said," Jules repeated, *"do you understand?"*

She wasn't sure how she did it. The words came out as more than words, almost something physical, like stones or arrows. They curled up from that endless sea of anger, at Simon and Jenny and at her shitty dad, at the passage of time and how it warped things, at the Piggly Wiggly monsters and the world that let them hurt whoever it thought was expendable. All that rage, but it was justified. It meant something, could be used for something.

She wouldn't let it be *eaten.*

The light flickered. The dark figure in it did too. Slowly, it faded from existence, taking the light with it. Darkness leached back, early-autumn night in scrubby pine forest, a girl with a twisted ankle and a broken wrist, a boy laced in mud and bruises.

"How did you do that?" Simon breathed.

"I don't know." Jules pulled away from him, started slowly up the hill. Absently, her hand rubbed against her sternum. Her anger was still there, potent, but she'd lost something when she'd used it like a weapon against the monster in the woods. It made her hollow, though the feeling wasn't necessarily *bad*.

"But the . . . the dreams," Simon stammered, eyes wide and casting around the trees like he thought someone was going to jump out of them and yell *surprise*. "Will they stop? I mean, my head feels clearer than it has in months, but—"

"They'll stop." Jules hissed through her teeth, pulled herself up the hill.

"How do you know?"

She turned. From her place on the embankment, she was taller than Simon was, looking down at him through the shadows.

"Because," she said quietly, "I'm pretty sure the monster in the woods is scared of me."

She didn't look back at him as she forced her way up the embankment, breathing hard against the pain in her ankle. The trees seemed to keep watch, an awareness in the air that had been there before, now magnified.

"Angry girl."

The words slithered on the wind, inhuman, coming from a mouth not made for language, a mouth that wasn't a mouth at all. Bloody and tired and broken, Jules stopped.

"It will only grow here. Your rage. There is so much in the world to be angry at." A cool breeze against her cheek. *"If you let me have it, it could be so much easier."*

"It's mine," Jules said. "You can't have it."

A pause. *"If you come with me, it could be easier."*

"I can't," she murmured, and fought down that needle point of temptation, swallowed it away.

"Then odds are," the monster of the Bridge whispered, *"that someday you will become something worse than I. Monsters are made, angry girl. They aren't born. I was like you once. My anger imprinted on the world, knit me into it once I passed from humanity and into something different."*

Jules snorted. Her ankle ached, her wrist was agony, but she still managed to lift up her other hand and shoot her middle finger at the darkened, whispering pines. "Then see you in a few decades, I guess."

No response. Slowly, the hum in the air quieted, until the night became nothing but chill and fog and night sky.

She turned and started trudging up the road.

Ghost on the Shore

by Allison Saft

*I*T'S A HOT NIGHT. I'M SITTING IN MY CAR, A CAMRY FIXING TO TAKE its last gasping breath any day now. It's my fault, I know. The tire pressure light is on, as it has been for weeks. The air conditioner died some forty miles outside Austin. And I never got the oil change I was supposed to before taking this road trip somebody might have talked me out of had I told anybody I was doing it. The thing is, I can't bring myself to worry about any of it. I'm not particularly attached to living these days.

Life is too fragile to get attached to. One day you're there, and the next, you're not. Summers here have a way of teaching you that. In summer, everything always teeters on that knife's edge of living and dying. There are the wildflowers opening up to an unforgiving sun. There are flies swarming a roadkill armadillo. There are the worms baked onto the sidewalk the morning after the season's only rain. And then there's me, parked in front of Iris Lake, where the dead stumble up from its depths. In Texas, it's one of those things you just know, the same as you know bluebonnets bloom in March and the moon pulls the tides. I don't remember the first time I heard the story: whether it was from my grandmother or a girl at recess or a babysitter. We all know that in some places, the dead don't stay dead.

A thick fog rolls in and paints my windshield a milky gray. Iris Lake stretches out before me like a dark handprint pressed into the earth. The water is a solid, ruthless black tonight. On its surface, the reflection of the trees crowd in toward the center of the lake with hungry, reaching fingers. Cold moonlight cuts across it like a vein of silver. The clock on my dashboard blinks 2:00 a.m., the time when it happens. My heart somersaults in my chest, and something like hope catches in my throat. I feel completely stupid for it. Sometimes I think maybe I really have lost it like everyone says I have. Only someone crazy would drive four hours just to sit by a lake in the middle of the night. Only someone crazy would hope to see the dead.

I fold myself up tighter in the driver's seat and watch moonlight ripple on the lake. I wait with my shallow breath going stale in my lungs. The air feels heavy with some kind of magic and my own heady anticipation. But as the minutes tick by, the tentative hope that sparked within me dies to ashes, and the reality I've tried so hard to deny slips back in.

June is gone.

Rationally, I know this. But I let myself get swept away by a silly story I was desperate enough to believe. I rest my forehead against my knees and take one breath, then another, until it feels less like my head is swimming. I concentrate on the feeling of sweat sliding beneath my collar, the scratch of linen against my skin. I inhale the scents of decaying reeds and wet earth. And I search for the high, pulsing drone of the crickets—only because they've abruptly stopped singing. Only the hum of my engine cuts up the night's uneasy silence. I lift my head, straining to listen to the night-sounds of the lake.

Something slams into the passenger-side window.

I startle so badly, I knock my knees into the steering wheel. "Jesus Christ."

But when I turn to look out the window, no one and nothing is there. There's only the shape of a handprint in the condensation caked on the window. Water trickles down the glass like the slow bleed of a wound. It looks somehow obscene in its impossibility, like a tear in the world I want to stitch shut. I touch my own hand to it, and when I smear the fog away, there's a dark shape, blurrily outlined.

Although I can't see their face clearly, I can feel their eyes boring into me with an intensity that makes the back of my neck prickle. Some part of me knows I should throw the car in reverse and drive. But that part of me has lain quiet for a long time. I roll down the window, and what I see hurts like a knife shoved between my ribs.

June.

She's wearing a white sundress that's dripping from the hem and plastered to her like a second skin. Beneath it, the straps of her swimsuit are a lurid purple against her collarbone. She's always been pale white, but she seems to glow now. There's something insubstantial about her, like all of her edges have been smudged with a careless hand.

"I'm so sorry to bother you." June's voice is like the pull of the lake against the shore. The sound fills me with an animal terror. "Could I get a ride please?"

Drive. The thought steals into my mind. There's something *wrong* with the girl standing at the passenger-side window, and everything in me rears back from her. My fingers tighten around the gear shift. But no matter how she sounds, no matter how she looks, it's still her. And if I leave now, I will never get to say my piece. That's a pain I already know, and it's far worse than the vague dread I feel right now.

"Yeah." By some miracle, my voice doesn't waver. "Get in."

June smiles softly. It's so polite, it's almost cold. In her horrible, crocodilian voice, she says, "Thank you."

I don't want her to speak ever again. I want her to talk to me for hours. My heart hammers in my throat as she opens the back door and climbs in as though moving through water. She doesn't buckle herself in, only sits there with her shoulders hunched forward and her hair hanging around her face in limp, knotted strands. It's caked in mud, like she's been dredged from the silt at the bottom of the lake. The smell of lake water is overpowering, briny and tinged with something sickly sweet like rot. I almost gag at the stench of it, but I swallow down my horror.

For her, I can do this.

My mouth opens and closes, but no sound comes out. For a year, all I could think about was what I'd give to see her one more time. All the things I never got to say. I was such a coward back when she was alive. Maybe I'm still a coward now, if I can't tell her even in death.

June doesn't seem to mind my silence. Like I'm a stranger to her or a rideshare driver, she says, "Could you drop me at 1227 Magnolia?"

"Sure," I rasp. "No problem."

It takes me way longer than it should to plug the address into my phone because I'm shaking so hard, I can barely type. Because I can *feel* her eyes like a blade on the back of my skull. The pin finally appears on the map, just about twenty minutes away. Somehow I manage to pull myself together enough to back the car onto the road. The darkness is so heavy, it falls over us like a curtain, and there are no streetlights to push it back. I take it slow around the bends, my hands white-knuckled around the wheel. The radio cuts in and out as a Top 40 station determinedly crackles through the static. Still, all I really hear is the steady pattering of June's wet hair on the seats. All I hear is her breath hissing and lurching through her chattering teeth.

We continue on that way for a few horrible minutes. Her hair drips, the static roars, and the longer she stares at me, the more I want to crawl out of my skin. The knob of my spine she's fixated on feels *alive*, seething with insects I know aren't there. I almost ask if she's okay, but it feels like an insensitive question. There are so many other things I want to ask anyway. So many things I want to say. But I start with something safe. "I've really missed you, you know."

She says nothing. It's almost unbearable to have vulnerability met with silence. I can't remember the last time I even tried.

"Okay." It comes out entirely more pathetic than I meant it to. "We don't have to talk, I guess."

June's breath comes in deepening, throatier gasps, as though she can't get enough air. Finally I dare to look back at her in the rearview. She's clutching her arms and rocking gently back and forth, shivers racking her body.

"Maud?" She sounds far away, underwater.

"What is it?" I say, too quickly.

"Please." For the first time since she appeared, she meets my eyes. I expect the steady blue of the San Marcos River. But they're a solid, lightless black, like the depths of the lake we left behind. They fill me up with cold. "Help me."

"Help you?" I choke out. "What?"

Water runs down her face and dribbles down her lips. Her eyes grow rounder, panicked.

Help me help me help me help me

The plea sounds as though it's inside my skull, horrible and shrill like metal grinding against metal. The rational part of me says, *Stop the car.* But I can't pull myself away from her stare. I don't feel entirely in control of myself as I press harder on the gas pedal. The engine revs. The condensation on my windshield thickens and streams down the glass in rivulets. I fumble with the wipers just as a muffled voice cuts through the radio's static. I mash the off button, but I still hear it like a drone in my head.

"What can I do? What else can I do?" I'm nearly shouting now as I meet her eyes in the rearview. "I can't drive any faster. I don't know what you want."

I realize too late that I've swerved out of the lane. A car horn blares. Headlights flood through the windshield. Instinct kicks in, and I sharply pull off the road, slamming on the brakes just before we crash into the guardrail. The other driver leans on the horn as they speed by.

"Fuck," I whisper, pressing my forehead to the steering wheel.

I'm glad that I can't see their expression. I'm even more glad that they can't see *mine*. I'm shivering, I realize, so hard that I feel like I'm going to rattle out of my skin. Sweat beads on my temples, and my heart beats a vicious *thud-thud* in every pulse point of my body. In the mirror, I look like a wreck. My lips are ghostly pale, my eyes wide and bloodshot. But over my shoulder, I see something much worse. My back seat is empty.

June is gone again.

It's very possible I've lost it.

I'm not thinking very clearly, I'm exhausted after the drive, and—as everyone is so fond of reminding me—grief does strange things to us. If I have to hear that one more time, I think I'll scream. I'm not discounting the possibility that I imagined everything. But the thing is, the back seat of my car is still soaked through. It still smells like lake water.

The earthiness of it once made me think of happier times: carefree summers floating in the river or rowing out to the center of Lady Bird Lake. June and I would lie flat on our backs, staring up at the pitiless sky, trading sips of the beer she'd convinced her older sister to buy for us. I wonder what about those dreamy afternoons—about *me*—lost its appeal for her. Why wasn't I enough to keep her from going to Iris Lake? Why hadn't I gone with her? Now, as I breathe in the stench of the water, I can only think of June's eyes when I met them in the mirror.

Bottomless. Horrible.

I don't want to think about it anymore, but I can't stop turning over last night when none of it makes sense. Legend has it that anyone who dies in Iris Lake's waters is kept sleeping beneath the surface. Every morning at two, the souls of the dead wash up on the shore and wait for someone to take them home. But June lived in Austin, not here. Why would she ask me to take her somewhere twenty minutes away from the lake?

I rub my eyes and take another sip of the coffee I'm nursing. This morning, I holed up in a coffee shop called the Peachtree Café. It's a charming spot, named, I assume, for the peaches that grow in the area. They've got all sorts of themed items on the laminated menu: peach cobblers, peach pies, peach muffins, peach salsa for the lunchtime crowd. Plants are crammed into every possible corner, on every possible surface, and even hang from the rafters. I've got a muffin on my plate torn half to shreds, which I almost feel guilty about. But I don't remember the last time I've really thought about food enough to be hungry.

Maybe *this* is finally rock bottom: a coffee shop in Nowhere, Texas. But every time I think that, I keep falling and falling into a lightless place like June's eyes. If there is a bottom to the way I feel, I don't intend to ever find it.

It's earlier than most people are awake, but it's already hot, with sunlight spilling over the tiled floor. I really should be asleep, but after dropping off June, I felt like a live wire.

Alive.

It's been a long time since I've felt alive or like myself, assuming there's anything left of myself after June took part of me with her to the grave. At school, I'm not really Maud anymore. I'm the dead girl's friend. I'm "troubled." I don't blame them for what they say about me. I *did* smash the windshield of Tanner Bolton's truck the day after June's funeral. I recognize now that it might've been extreme, but here's how it is. One day, June tells me she's going to Tanner's lake house over spring break. Another, her mom calls me up and says that she's gone.

Drowned. Her voice was so garbled, I thought maybe *I* was the one underwater. *A horrible accident.*

It isn't fair. It isn't fucking fair that Tanner Bolton draws breath and June none at all. So I smashed his window. It was worth every disappointed look my parents gave me.

"Can I get you anything else?"

"Huh?"

"Anything else you need?" The girl standing at my elbow carries a pot of coffee and, apparently, the entire weight of the world on her shoulders. She exudes the smell of cigarette smoke and a practiced aura of ennui. She's distractingly pretty, even though she's looking at me like I'm a sad little insect. Her brown hair is tied back in a sleek ponytail, and her skin is the color of sandstone. "Something else to shred? Some paper, maybe?"

As I blink the sun out of my eyes, I see that she's my age. The name tag on her apron says, *Need anything? I'm happy to provide you service excellence! My name is Carolina.* Between her unimpressed glare and the all-black getup beneath her apron, I kind of doubt she'd be happy to do much of anything. I curl myself around my mug and mutter, "Sorry. Thanks. I'm good for now."

"Right. So, what brings you to town?"

"I heard the food was good."

She stares down at my full cup and ritualistically disassembled muffin. "I see we've disappointed."

"No, I'm just . . ." I sigh. I feel like I owe her something now, so I tell her the truth. "I'm here to see Iris Lake."

Her spine straightens. "Oh yeah? Well, no good comes from that lake."

"I know it. It took my friend."

I don't know why I say it. Lately I don't know why I do or say half the things I do. There's something vindicating about the shock on people's faces. I like to see how they try to recover the conversation. I like to see them squirm.

Carolina doesn't even blink. "It won't give them back, either."

It already has, I want to say, but I'm ready for this conversation to be over. I bite my tongue and shrug instead.

Carolina has no interest in sparing me, however. She glances over her shoulder and surveys the empty café. The old-timey jukebox crackles merrily in the corner, but now that I'm listening, I can make out the steady *drip, drop, drip* of water. I can't figure out where it's coming from. How had I not noticed it before? Every drop sounds as loud as gunfire.

Carolina sets down the pot of coffee and slides into the seat across from me. I don't like the look she's giving me. I see it all the time on my therapist. And before they stopped talking to me, I saw it on my friends when they told me I needed to get my life together and "do the bare minimum." It's a look that expects something from you. But I don't have anything left to give.

"I'm going to give you some advice. No extra charge." There is no room for argument in her tone. "What's your name?"

"Maud."

"Okay, Maud." It's a surprisingly nice sound, my name on her lips. She has the barest hint of a West Texas accent. "I get it. All of us have to see Iris Lake for ourselves at least once. But what you saw . . . It may look like your friend, but it's not."

I can't describe the feeling that slithers through me then. It's something like rage and something like relief. I feel out of control, and it's made worse by that awful sound. The *drip, drop, drip* of some pipe I can't see. I look up. Carolina follows my gaze to the ceiling.

"If it's not her, then what is it?" I know I sound cruel when I say it.

"The Lady of the Lake." There are no theatrics in her voice, no campfire flair.

"The Lady of the Lake," I repeat incredulously.

Carolina catches herself just before she rolls her eyes. It reminds me so much of June that it almost takes the breath out of me. "Laugh all you want. All I know is that it's best to get in your car and drive back to wherever you came from. All right?"

Drip, drop, drip. Each droplet seems to shatter inside my skull. "There's nothing for me back where I came from."

"No," she says sharply. "No, see, that's not an answer. Come up with a better one. You have to find something. And in the meantime, if you see it again, you have to tell it to go."

It. I bristle. "What the hell do you know anyway?"

"A lot. You can go through life like this, or you can make an effort to move on." She gestures to her uniform. "Do you think I want to be here? It keeps me busy, and it keeps me out of the house."

The way she says *house*, like it's more of an entity than a place, speaks to me. But I can't let up until I make Carolina understand. I have to talk to June. I have to tell her what I couldn't tell her in life—what I couldn't tell *anyone*. "This *is* moving on. I'm trying to say goodbye to her. And last night, she . . . She's trying to get me to take her somewhere. She's trying to tell me something. I know it, and if I can just figure out what it is—"

"Listen to me, Maud, or don't. I don't care." Carolina presses her hands flat against the table. "The dead are dead. She doesn't have any unfinished business. You're the one keeping her here, and that's like an anchor to the thing on the other side of that lake."

I'm breathing heavily. She is too. For a moment I see myself reflected in her eyes. We're wearing the same hollowed-out expression.

Drip, drop, drip. I feel something wet plop onto the top of my head. At first, I have the ridiculous thought that it's blood. But it's so cold, and I realize it's water carving a line down the back of my neck. Carolina's gaze is unwavering. Her eyes are as dark as lake water.

"You have to let her go," she says.

But that's just the thing. I can't.

After baking in the sun for a while, my car smells like decay and damp leather. Even in the midmorning sun, I'm cold—or maybe I'm just anxious. Either way, I crank up the heat as high as it will go and wait for my teeth to stop chattering.

No matter what Carolina says, I can't let this go. I won't. She didn't experience what I did. The desperation in June's voice. The look in her eyes when she begged me to help her.

It's a long way off from two a.m., but I can't just sit here. Maybe if I can find what June wants at 1227 Magnolia, she'll actually talk to me instead of begging for my help. I slide my phone out of my pocket and plug it in. When it finally flickers to life, my notifications—or lack thereof—are a reflection of how depressing my life has become. I've got nothing but a text from my mom, a cursory check-in, and an email from the coffee shop down the street from my house. I don't bother replying to my mom; instead I type the address into my GPS. The sharp edges of my broken screen dig into the pad of my thumb with a bright pain I hardly feel.

It's weird to be driving on this road at this time of day, skirting the edge of Iris Lake. Right now there's nothing at all eerie or magical about it. The grass is like straw, stiff and brown from the unrelenting heat. The lattice of branches overhead is blanched and skeletal in the sunlight. Worst of all is the lake itself, half burned away by drought. I can see new islands breaching the surface; they'd been hidden last night beneath a cloak of mist. I dread to think of what they'd find at the bottom if the lake ran dry for good. Maybe all those ghosts would be unleashed—or the Lady of the Lake herself.

I can't believe I'm even entertaining Carolina's warning.

It takes only fifteen minutes to arrive at a neighborhood. It's not a gated community, but I can tell it aspires to be. The houses aren't perfectly identical, but they're all made of the same freckled stone, their lawns manicured to some homeowner association's exacting standards. The grass is a startling green that screams, *Water rations don't apply here!* It all looks foreboding, its polish as good as a Keep Out sign. I think again of the way Carolina spat out the word *house* like a mouthful of glass.

I roll to a stop in front of 1227 Magnolia and throw the car in park. The house is just like the others, all imposing white stone and stately plantation shutters. I don't know what I expected, if I'm being honest. If this place matters enough to June to possess her even in death, maybe I thought I'd see something of her in it: warmth or light or *anything*. A half-naked tree sways softly in the breeze. All the leaves must've dropped off in the freeze two years ago, because new growth sprouts awkwardly beneath the bare branches. The windows are all dark, revealing nothing of the inside.

All of a sudden I feel sick. What the hell am I doing here at some stranger's house? Maybe Carolina was right. I have no business being here. I should just turn around and drive back home.

Maud, please. June's voice blooms in my mind like blood dropped into water. *Help me.*

No, this is insane. I'm not doing anything wrong. I'm just asking if they knew her. I draw in a breath and shake myself to get the nerves out. Then I stride to the front door with as much confidence as I can muster. A trellis of passionflower vines climbs up the siding, their blooms strangely bright and alien. Bees swarm them, and a cloud of gnats eddies around my ankles like a pool of water. What strikes me the most, though, is the patio furniture. It's tidy and white with aggressive floral cushions and an air that invites you to imagine a wooden sign above it that says something like, "Lord, bless this home with love and laughter." Everything is *just so*, except for an unemptied ashtray on the table and a tin can full of cigarette butts. I decide I like whoever they belong to.

I knock on the door. Within seconds a massive dog appears in the window, bellowing at me. Then I see the woman behind it. Even before she opens the door, I feel the slap of her judgment. She frowns at me, barely opening the door enough to poke her head out. She looks strangely familiar, but I can't exactly place her. She has sleek brown hair cropped close to her ears and a stare that could cut through steel. Maybe the love-and-laughter sign would've been a good addition to the décor after all. She could certainly use the reminder.

"Can I help you?" she asks.

I realize, probably too late, I didn't exactly think this through. What am I going to say? *Hey, my dead friend wants to be dropped off at your house. Do you know why that might be?* I clear my throat. "I'm sorry to bother you, but I was wondering if you knew someone named June Mahoney."

Recognition lights her eyes. They burn with a steady, cold fire. "No. I'm sorry."

Something within me cracks. She's lying to me. I swear I hear it again. That *drip, drop, drip* getting louder with every beat against the stone patio. "I know that's not true."

Her dog barks again, a deep rumbling one that almost has me leaping back from the door. "Excuse me?"

This time she sounds offended, but I can't bring myself to care. "You're lying to me."

"I think you should leave."

"I know you know who June is." I hear my own voice rising above the drip of the water. I feel that old urge in me, the same one that had possessed me to take a rock to Tanner Bolton's truck. "Why else would she give me this address?"

The woman fixes me with a look of plain shock. She looks as though she wants to snap something back at me, but whatever she sees in my face must make her think better of it. "I don't want you or your friends coming around my daughter anymore. Next time I'll call the police."

She slams the door in my face, and for a moment all I can think is, *I deserved that.* The next thing I think is, *Daughter?*

Not that it matters. I've blown any chance I had at getting more answers from her. I trudge back to my car, my face burning. It's not just embarrassment. It's anger and shame and a thousand other things I haven't let myself feel. I try to shove them down as hard as I can. I slam the lid of my mind over them and chain it shut. But I can't stem the tide. All of my insulation has been peeled off.

This was pointless. This whole trip was completely pointless.

Unless I want to stake out this house or hunt down that woman's daughter, I've hit a wall. Or maybe I imagined that look in her eyes altogether. I can't trust myself anymore. Maybe there's some other significance of this place that I can't even begin to guess at. Something June had kept for herself. That's what hits me the hardest: that I don't *know.*

In the months before she died, June moved through the world like she was carrying a secret. She was always on her phone, smiling as she texted and turning it facedown on the table. She walked more lightly, as though she might lift off from the earth in the slightest breeze. And when she told me she was going on that trip to Iris Lake, she'd practically glowed with excitement. Something was waiting for her here. June had a life outside of me. It hurts, sharp as a wound, to realize that as close as we were, I didn't know everything about June. And now I never will.

Not unless I get her to talk to me.

I pull out my phone. I've got about ten missed calls and voicemails from both of my parents now. Without listening to them, I delete every single one. I don't want to be scolded. I don't want to lose my nerve. And deep down, maybe I don't want to hurt them any more than I already have. It'll make it harder on them if they believe there was ever a shot at saving me. I'm already long gone. And there's only one thing left for me to do.

When the witching hour falls and the pale mist lifts off the lake like a veil, I'm waiting for June to arrive. The night is still and hot, and I have my windows cracked open to listen to the pull of the lake, its waves sloshing against the shore. And because I know what to watch for, this time I see her arrive.

Wisps of mist rise into the night, so faint that it could be a trick of the sallow moonlight. But through the reeds, I see her. She emerges from the water like a wraith, dripping from the ends of her hair, the fabric of her dress soaked through and streaked with mud. It clings to every curve of her body.

When she locks eyes with me, the temperature plummets. The sweat on my skin feels clammy, like another, ill-fitting skin. She does not break eye contact as she approaches my car, her footsteps a wet slap against the sand. Tonight she looks more solid than she did before. And this time she gets in without asking.

She settles into the back seat and doesn't say a single word.

I glance at her in the rearview and immediately wish I hadn't. Her hair lifts gradually from the back of her neck, drifting upward as though the car were filling with water. It coils against the roof like seaweed swaying in the current. She stares at me, and I force myself to stare back at her. Her eyes are like portals to the bottom of that lake. The longer I look, the more I get the impression I'm not looking at *her* but at something else that's peering out from within her skull. Every ounce of self-preservation left in me shrieks, a snared-rabbit sound.

I have to get out of here.

But when I blink, her sharklike eyes are placid as still water.

"Are you going to say anything to me?" I ask, hating how small my voice sounds.

She doesn't reply.

Well, 1227 Magnolia it is, then. I back us out of the lot, onto the road. From the corner of my eye, I watch the rhythmic twining and knotting of her hair. June presses her hand to the window, as if she wants to get out. The glass immediately blooms with condensation. The temperature drops even further, and my breath clouds in the air. The trees loom out of the fog, reaching for us as we whiz by.

June's vacant gaze is reflected in the window. It fills me with loneliness as deep as the day she left this world. She looks so little like herself right now. With every passing moment, dread coils tighter within me. I'd hoped this would be . . . I don't know, healing, maybe. But instead I feel like a glorified chauffer for someone who doesn't even want to be here. The ridiculous, petty smallness of that feeling makes me irritable, of all things.

"I went there earlier today. I asked the woman who lived there if she knew who you were, but she didn't. I think she was lying, because she seemed pretty pissed off when I said your name." When she doesn't reply, I say, "What'd you do to her?"

June strikes the window with the flat of her palm, startling me. I want to scream with frustration. I want to shake answers loose from her. But how can I argue with someone who won't even speak? I tighten my grip on the steering wheel.

"What do you want, June?"

Silence. Again.

The speedometer surges with my anger. I'm so sick of this.

I'm so sick of playing this game with her. Suddenly I can't hold it back any longer. Some tether has bound us together, and I'll be damned if I don't try to pull on it.

"Well, do you know what *I* want? I want to stop being a fucking coward. I kept thinking I was ready to tell you, over and over again, for *years*. But every time I got the thought in my head, I'd chicken out. And then last year I was finally ready. I was planning on telling you as soon as you got back from the trip, but I never got the chance. On top of everything, I felt so stupid. Like I had wasted every day with you I'd ever been given. What was there to be afraid of when . . ."

When you died.

I choke out a bitter laugh. It comes out half a whimper. For a moment I think I'm going to chicken out again. But what am I protecting myself from anymore? All my friends abandoned me to my grief. My parents probably think I'm already dead since I'm screening their calls, and hell, at the rate the trees are blurring past us now, with one wrong move I will be. The fog is so dense tonight, it makes it seem as though we're underwater.

There is nothing else for me to lose.

"So when I remembered the stories about Iris Lake, I thought this was it. Some twist of fate, a second chance. So here it is, whether you want to hear it or not. I've been trying to work up the courage to tell you that I'm in love with you."

Finally admitting it breaks open something within me. It

feels like lancing a wound and letting the poison run out. But the words fall between us, impotent. This time, silence is not what I expect. My breath shudders out of me.

"I love you, June," I repeat. "Losing you was more than I could take. It's been a year, and I don't know how to survive it. What am I supposed to do? How am I supposed to get over you?"

She strikes the window again, this time with the side of her closed fist.

"Do you even care?" I ask. "Can you even hear me?"

I dare to look at her again in the mirror. Her stare is unbroken on mine. There is something intent in that stare. Something baleful, almost hateful. It stuns me, snatching my breath away like I've plunged into freezing waters. June Mahoney was many things, not all of them good. But she wasn't cruel. The June I knew would never ignore someone hurting. Even during our worst fights, she would never look at me like this.

She breathes into the silence. Each breath is thick and rattling, as if she is struggling to inhale through lungfuls of mud. Each one sounds different. One like the growl of an alligator, another like the wheeze of a sickly child. I'm frozen with my hands on the steering wheel. Condensation drips down the glass in thick rivulets. The water *drip, drop, drips* from her hair in a steady rhythm.

What you saw . . . It may look like your friend, but it's not.

For the first time, I start to believe Carolina. Any relief I felt at my confession evaporates into mist. There is no one here to hear it. June who is not June stares at me in the mirror with an expression that does not belong on her face. It's hideous and full of hunger. The reality I've tried so long to deny closes in on me. June is gone, and nothing is going to give her back to me.

Pound goes her fist against the glass. *Pound, pound, pound.*

The glass shudders, then splinters.

Fear twists my stomach. "What are you?"

The glass gives way entirely. Water floods in, spilling over my seats, sloshing into the footwell. It rushes in quicker than I could've imagined, like I've driven us headlong into the lake. I feel it rise around my ankles. The brackish smell of it, of decay, overwhelms me. Before I can even process it, not-June lurches forward and struggles to get her hands around my throat.

I try to throw her off, and the car veers into the other lane. I scrabble at the wheel as she scrabbles at my neck, her nails biting into my skin. June screams, a vicious, inhuman sound that sets my blood to ice. But I scream louder. Everything I've kept inside, all the rage and the loneliness, it's all pouring out of me now. This goddamn lake took her from me, and it gave me back *this*.

The Lady of the Lake.

June is gone. I repeat it like a mantra. Because if I refuse to accept it—if I refuse to let her go—it's going to kill me one way or another. June is gone, and the last piece of me that clung to her is gone too. I don't know what's left of me, after her death hollowed me out. But right now all I know is that I don't want to fucking die here. I don't want to die like this.

I don't want to die.

The Lady gets a better hold on me and squeezes. Her flesh is yielding against mine, like it's waterlogged and flaking, but she's strong. I can't struggle without jerking the wheel. But if I continue on like this, I'm going to crash the car, and—

And she isn't wearing her seat belt.

"Get off me!"

Before I can talk myself out of it, I slam on the brakes. I close my eyes as the wheels lose traction. Everything seems to happen in slow motion. There's a sickening *crunch* of metal, the piercing ring of shattering glass, the inhuman wail of the thing wearing June's face. I'm thrown forward into the airbag, and pain bursts in my skull. My vision goes black.

I feel my chest heaving with my frantic breaths, but I can't hear a thing over the tinny ringing in my ears. For a moment I'm not sure if the car is still moving—if *I'm* still moving. I touch my face and my hands come away soaked—but with water, not with blood. I almost sob with relief. My heart beats, pumping rage and sorrow through me in equal measure. But they're bright and vivid as the blood roaring through me.

Alive. I'm alive.

With shaking hands, I unclasp the seat belt and crawl out of

the car. A wave of water sloshes out after me. I search the darkness for the Lady of the Lake, expecting to see her watching me
with those cruel eyes. But there's nothing in the guttering glow
of my headlights. There's nothing but shards of glass and water
reflecting the cold light of the streetlamps.

She's gone. She's really gone.

For the first time in a year I cry. They're deep, horrible sobs
that rack my whole body. Everything aches, and I know that I'm
probably going to be dragged to the hospital and forced to explain
the whole situation—along with the things I *can't* explain, like
why I'm soaked to the bone and why I crashed my car completely
sober. But right now I can't bring myself to worry about it. Right
now I'm free.

All around me, the neighborhood begins to stir. Windows illuminate like candles blooming softly to life. Doors fly open, letting
out golden light from within. People stumble onto their porches,
squinting into the dark to see my totaled car and the disaster
of a girl who crashed it. I almost laugh. Somehow I made it to
Magnolia.

"Maud?" a familiar voice asks. "Oh my God, Maud, are
you okay?"

I look up to see Carolina standing over me. I smear the tear
tracks off my face as quickly as I can. "What are you doing here?"

Somehow it's the wrong thing to say. She looks at me, then at
the water spilling from my open car door and running down the

street. Her face scrunches up helplessly, as if she can't think of anything better to do than to answer my ridiculous question. She gestures behind her, right at 1227 Magnolia. "I live here. What are *you* doing here?"

My heart drops into my stomach. "You live at 1227 Magnolia?"

"Yes? I hardly see how that matters right now."

"It's you." My voice sounds oddly flat. "You're what she was looking for. June Mahoney."

At the sound of June's name, Carolina's expression crumples. Just like that, everything makes a horrible, perfect kind of sense. I think of June and her secret smiles. I think of her phone, face-down in the fraught space between us. I think of the woman at 1227 Magnolia and her tight-lipped rage. How did I not notice the resemblance between her and Carolina sooner? Maybe I've never seen a single thing clearly in my life if I didn't see this.

June was in love with this girl.

The closure I've wanted for so long guts me. Whether or not I'd found the courage to tell her how I felt, none of it would have mattered. Her heart already belonged to someone else. Embarrassment drives all the pain from my body. In its place, anger fills me up like lake water. If June hadn't gone to see Carolina, maybe she'd still be alive. Maybe I'd have been humiliated by her rejection, but at least I'd have been honest. At least I'd *know*.

"I'm sorry," Carolina says quietly. "You must hate me."

Yes. The word pools on my tongue like venom.

It would be so easy to blame her. It would be so easy to hurt her. I want to scream at her. I want to put a rock through her window. The worst, most self-pitying part of me wants to tear her apart. I want to know what it is that June saw in her, what she has that I don't. When I meet her eyes, it feels like staring at my own reflection. She looks at me like she's already resigned. Like she wants me to condemn her. I want to. I want to hate her.

But I can't.

At the end of it all, we're just two girls kneeling in the wreckage of our love.

Somewhere in the distance, I hear the scream of a siren rising into the night-like mist. Although it takes every ounce of strength I have left, I speak to her gently. I tell her what I wish I could believe about myself.

"Anyone she loved," I say, "can't be all bad."

Petrified

by Olivia Chadha

*T*HE FOREST WAS AWAKE. THE PINE TREES BENT DOWN CLOSER TO the edge of the parking lot as we walked to Will's car after the Friday night football game. It wasn't like last time. It didn't show itself after a storm in the old cottonwood that fell and smashed the gas station to bits. This time was different. This time the forest was hungry.

"Hey, wait up!" I said to Will and Jocelyn. In the rush, I slipped on the gravel and landed hard on one knee, sharp rocks slashing through my tights and into my skin. The navy night sky cast strange shadows from the forest that beckoned to me. The Aspen charm around my neck warmed between my forefinger and thumb. The same charm all Children of the Aspen wore.

"I've got ya, Dhara," Jocelyn said, giving me a lift. "That's what you get for wearing jean shorts and tights to a football game."

"Leave her alone. She looks cute," Will, Jocelyn's twin, said.

"It's true," I said. "I do. Or I did."

"Was it another dizzy spell?" Jocelyn asked. Something shifted in the forest. My skin was on fire. I nodded. Their faces flushed and then Will and Joce each touched their charms.

My parents were going to kill me. They never approved of short shorts with or without tights underneath. Their immigrant beliefs carried along with them when my grandparents immigrated to Colorado from India and joined the community. The blood trickled from the puncture wounds on my knee. Jean shorts weren't a good idea tonight. But the final autumnal burst of sun earlier in the day had convinced me to wear them. It was the equinox; the full sun gave light to the land and life just a bit longer today. Must have made me a little too confident.

The last massive group of rowdy kids jumped into the back of a pickup truck and sped away dangerously fast around the dark unlit mountain roads leading away from Ridgecrest High.

"Ravine?" I asked.

"Yeah, they can have the ravine." Will nodded.

"You know how I love watching drunk people shoot cans off fence posts," I said as we came to the beat-up old Subaru we called Chuck. Will had rebuilt Chuck from scraps at his family's auto shop in town.

"I'd like to keep my head attached to my neck, you know?" Jocelyn said, rubbing her hand to her throat, her blond hair falling around her shoulders in thick curls.

There was laughter and whistling and we all turned. Jackson was flanked by a couple of his lackeys. My skin crawled. Joce and Will stood between me and the approaching crew. They were already wasted.

Jackson ran into Will carelessly, like he expected everyone to get out of his way.

"Hey, watch it, dude," Will said, and pushed back.

One of the boys said my name as they passed. "Dhara. Dhara the Missing Girl. Are you still lost? Freak." They spit the last part.

"Come on guys," I said. "Let's get out of here."

I was used to the names that outsiders gave me and our group. "A Child Lost in the Woods" the headlines read. When I was five, I went missing for a month. My parents told me the phones rang off the hook asking about their lifestyle, the Children of the Aspen community we belonged to. They finally ripped the phone from the wall. But the detectives asked the wrong questions. My parents thought I was dead, eaten by a mountain lion or coyote, kidnapped, or drowned in the Barker Reservoir. I don't remember much because I was so young. There were feelings, sensations of dirt between my toes and under my fingernails, and being pulled under the earth, rooted down deep. I remember waking on my porch in my dirty nightgown, bark and dirt and tree branches tangled in my long black hair. This place had secrets, and we didn't tell outsiders about them. But that night years ago, the forest made a bargain with me.

As the group passed, Jackson's eyes lingered on me, and it was like the whole world froze.

He and his posse headed to his BMW, parked directly in front of us. He'd looked so special when I first saw him in his expensive car, like money made someone better. Jackson Tillman and his family were still new to this mountain town, even though he'd moved months earlier. New to this village where everyone else was born and raised. His family was new money in this old town, and like great colonizers who came to free the lowly people in a foreign land, they came here with big ideas. New to Colorado. But being new didn't excuse a person from knowing certain simple human things. Like most towns, there were rules about right and wrong, and this place was no different.

"I bet he loves that car more than anything," Will said too loudly as we slid into the Subaru. He checked his rearview mirror and tossed his keys into the glove box.

"Maybe. But not more than his father's bank account," Joce said, riding shotgun.

The wind picked up and blew a cloud of yellow Aspen leaves around our car. It felt like something was going to change, like the unusual heat of the day had disturbed the forest. Suddenly there were raised voices around Jackson's car. We all turned to witness the chaos. His friends hitched a ride in a different car, and he was left alone trying to turn over his engine again and again, lights flashing, nothing firing.

"Guys, I think he needs help," Will said.

"What do you say, Dhara?" Joce turned around and held my hand. We exchanged looks and all got out of the Subaru.

Will cranked the heat, popped his hood, pulled his jumper cables from the trunk. "Probably just needs a jump."

"What do you know about cars?" Jackson asked.

"I grew up working on them, so there's that. It just needs a jump. Happens all the time when the weather changes in high altitude."

"All right. Be careful not to scratch her," Jackson said.

Will attached the cables, and Jackson sat back in his car to push the ignition switch again. The engine *click-click*ed and did nothing.

"Crap!" Jackson yelled. The parking lot was now completely empty aside from us.

"It's dead. You need a new battery," Will said.

When Jackson got into the back seat, the first thing he said to me was, "Hey." Like we'd known each other forever. "Battery dead. Sucks." He was hypnotically gorgeous, every single tooth in place.

"Your friends just left you?" I asked.

"Their girlfriends are waiting at the ravine." He frantically swiped at his phone's screen. "Can't leave her parked here overnight."

"Dead zone, bro," Joce and Will said in unison.

I said, "No one's calling you, and you aren't calling anyone."

"What is up with this town?" He pouted.

"There's fun to be had if you know where to look." But he'd know that if he weren't from a city. City people who visit the mountains come here to buy local honey and feel better about nature and their connection to it. Then they head back to their lives, buy fast-fashion leggings, and return to being the self-centered people they were before. Don't get me wrong. I love cities. It's the tourists that kill me. Not everyone who visits is a tourist. Jackson was a tourist. Not really in his body. Just waiting to return to where he came from. He was like an invasive weed where a native plant should be. Incongruent and dangerous.

"Sure, okay," he said.

When he turned to face me, the harvest moonlight bathed his skin perfectly. He'd dodged all freckles, zits, and blemishes unlike the rest of humanity. Money can buy you some things.

"We have service at the cabin. It's not far. You can call for help or a ride from there. I'm not driving you all the way around the ridge to your estate." Will said it like it wasn't even a question. He was serving a fact. "That, or you can walk." Will pointed to the darkness of the forest surrounding us.

"Cool, cool. Thanks, man."

The drive was on a mostly dirt road. Our cabin had been our fort since we were little. Our parents, along with other families who belonged to our tightly knit Children of the Aspen community, purchased the open space to keep it undeveloped. On the one hundred acres was an outbuilding, open for use by anyone in the group. We were the only ones who used it regularly, though.

High peaks surrounded us like the shoulders of a tremendous monster. A copse of spindly white aspens lined both sides of the road like a dense white bone fence. Some trees were petrified, but that didn't mean they were dead. In fact, they were very much alive. Aspens were all connected, one of the largest living organisms on the planet. If you listened, they talked to each other. Talked about us. The thing about petrified forests was that they could be weigh stations for litterers and druggies, and curious people on cross-country road trips who also brought empty chip bags and gum stains. Our town never wanted to put up a billboard, wanted invisibility rather than infamy. So our community kept it quiet, sworn to secrecy. We knew the power within the trees. And we had to keep that safe.

"I'm just curious," Jackson said. His breath a gust of stale beer. "Is it true what they say about you guys?"

"What do they say?" I asked.

"That you're all into weird stuff like witches and occult."

He laughed.

"Nah, that's silly. There hasn't been a witch out here for centuries," Jocelyn said without a hint of humor. "I'm joking. We aren't witches, bro."

"So, what do you guys get into?" I felt Jackson's body move slightly closer to mine.

Joce turned toward him; her pink glossy lips glittered in the moonlight. "You're welcome to observe the locals if you're brave enough." She shook her black flask at him, teasingly.

"I'm in," he said.

She passed it to him, and he took a swig without asking what was inside.

"Do you like games, Jackson?" I asked.

It was the heat. Last summer's scorching weather got into everything. It weighed in our lungs, swelled the wood floorboards, made my skin sticky with sweat. Joce said the town went mad from it. The hot Chinook winds kicked up roof tiles and sent trees into house windows, downed power lines, and kept everyone awake at night with banshee-like screaming. Out here in the Rockies it was never that hot; most houses didn't even have air-conditioning. That's why Will and Joce and I decided we needed to hitch a ride to Grand Lake to swim. It was a two-hour drive and Will's Subaru was in the shop, overheated, smoking, coughing up a lung.

We hitched with our backpacks and tent. Headed up along the Peak to Peak Highway. The Children of the Aspen elders gave us Fridays off in the summers after we finished our chores. I was picky about the cars that kept stopping for us. Some trucks were too crowded. Others had a few guys who didn't look safe. Finally, a shiny new BMW cruised up alongside us. Jackson was alone in his car, going for a drive. His car looked so tempting and air-conditioned.

"Where you guys going?" he asked. I remembered him from English class.

"Grand Lake. Wanna come?" Joce said.

"Yeah, sure. Hop in." It was easy. Too easy.

He asked me to sit in the front. I'd never been in a car that nice before. He put his hand lazily by my leg and I let him. It felt different, exciting. A few miles into our drive, we passed a white wooden memorial cross, twisted with plastic flowers and sun-bleached garlands. "Y'all religious here or what?" Jackson asked.

We all looked at each other. Joce took the lead. "Some people died in there. In the forest. Some serial killer or something."

"Did they ever find who did it?" Jackson said.

"Nah, they did it to themselves," Will said. "I mean, they got lost and crossed into the thicket. It's hard to find your way out sometimes. People get turned around."

"Thicket?" he asked.

Joce said, "It's just a ghost story. What we call the thickest part of the forest. That, or the forest is cursed."

Matt Harkel, Simon Duda, Jamie Francis. No one knew what they were doing. A few years back they decided to camp on our open space. Lit matches and shot cans off tree stumps with a .45 that was impossible to aim. Just jerks who'd get shit-faced, hurt defenseless animals, bully children, violate the land. Their bodies were found in a pile, stacked neatly on top of one another, like the cairns surrounding them, twisted wood through them all. The local police searched for a murderer for years. Case went cold.

"Creepy. I like nature in small doses. This is a little much for me. But my dad has plans for this town. So it shouldn't be long."

"Right, he's opening a new mercantile?" I asked.

He gave me a cheesy smile. "Yeah, and a mall, a park, a bike park, restaurants, and hotels. The whole nine. It's going to be a next-level resort area. People will come from all over to check it out. I mean, look at that view of the Rockies. It's amazing."

"Can you pull over?" My hand pressed against my mouth. "I think I'm going to be sick." I twisted the charm around my neck three times and took three deep breaths.

Joce and Will sipped their flask on the two-hour drive while Jackson and I waited until we got to the Grand Lake beach. We swam. It was heaven. My long black hair was wavy from the water, and my tan skin soaked up the sun. The cold mountain lake gave us life. We got sandwiches from the stand and shared them. Ice cream afterward. We watched the sun go behind the mountains and let our toes twist and tangle in the sand. We decided to camp, and after Joce and Will passed out in the tent, I ducked out to look at the stars. It was so dark in the infinite Milky Way, and nebulas and stars and planets felt within my reach. The sky reflected on the placid lake, a mirror of eternity.

Jackson kissed me then. I wasn't drunk, just really tired. I don't think he was either. A kiss was new and fun and exhilarating. It wasn't my first, but it was new, and the day had been a gift. That's all I wanted. A kiss. Under the stars.

But he didn't care. He didn't listen.

And that's why.

The cabin's stairs ached as we walked to the front door and unlatched it. Tree branches twisted around the old one-room structure like they were begging to come in, to reclaim it. I stroked the vines that flourished around the doorway; they shivered under my fingertips.

Will lit the lanterns and tossed some salvaged beetle-kill wood into the old woodburning stove, not for heat, for light.

"What is this place?" Jackson asked. "Looks haunted." His

words were growing lazy; he'd had a few sips from the flask already. Maybe he forgot about his car, his phone. Joce's special fermented herbal cocktail wasn't for the faint of heart.

"Home," I said.

Jackson inspected the oil paintings and framed photographs of the Children of the Aspen founders that hung on the walls. "Family photos?" he asked.

"Local history." I traced my finger over the black-and-white photograph of the founders with their families chained to the last few trees in Riverbend Gulch. "Hundreds of trees had been cut down by a company to make timber for houses. They stood up to protect the forest."

"Whoa. What happened?"

We all looked at each other. "They died. It was for the greater good."

Jackson's mouth opened to say something, but I left him there without an audience.

Jocelyn said, all bubbly, "Ready to play, guys?"

"Sure. What's the game?" He edged closer to me. "Truth or Dare? Never Have I Ever?" He laughed and I wanted to press my hand over his mouth and make him stop.

"Hide-and-seek," Will and Joce said in unison.

A smile stretched across Jackson's face. "Really? That sounds basic."

I lined up glasses on the table and filled each with two shots of Joce's homemade brew. "Rules are, there's one seeker. The three others hide. If it takes the seeker more than five minutes to find the hiders, the seeker has to drink. If they find the hiders early, the hiders have to drink the whole glass. Got it?"

"Yeah, got it. Sounds easy."

"Bro, you're going to love this," Will said, and hit Jackson on the arm a little harder than friendly.

"Let's draw sticks to decide who's the seeker. Short stick is it," I said. With my back turned, I placed the pine sticks of different sizes in my hand. "You first, Will." Will pulled a medium twig. Jocelyn pulled another similar in size. Jackson paused and took in the remaining two branches, and drew a shorter one, leaving me the longest one of all.

"Looks like you're it, bro," said Joce.

Jackson put his hand on my shoulder. "I'll be gentle."

"Close your eyes, Jacks," I said pointedly, remembering he hated when people shortened his name. He bristled.

"Remember, we could be anywhere in the area. Count to twenty and then come outside, okay? And no cheating."

"One, two . . ." Jackson's voice trailed off.

The three of us left the cabin, cups in hand, and headed deeper into the petrified aspen grove. On a fall night like this, it didn't look as dark and frightening as it usually did, at least not to me. Its petrified trees frozen in broken angles, bark as hard as rock, branch edges sharp as knives opened up to us, drew us in farther. But this forest was alive. Everyone in the community knew that. And now Jackson would know.

Joce and Will went behind the center of the petrified forest, and I stood downhill near a small group of trees and waited. There was only an ancient square rock border remaining of the old inn that had burned down centuries earlier. Inside grew the oldest aspen tree grove in the area; white with permanently yellowed leaves even in the summer, it was the center of everything. A thick bramble and chaotic grape vines wound around the tree trunks.

Something stung my leg. A splinter imbedded under my skin in the wound I'd managed earlier. A tender green spiral of vine emerged from my wound. The trees were telling me it was time.

His footsteps cracked across tree branches carelessly. The grasshoppers' symphonic melody carried on the crisp evening air, surrounding us. Jackson called, "Dhara? Dhara, are you there?"

I hoped my laugh was enough to draw him closer.

"Hey, wait up. It's dark out here," he said.

Right when he got close, I moved into the woods. "You know that trees have memories?"

His footsteps weren't far. "Dhara?"

"Come on, Jackson, you have to find me."

"I'm coming," he said, laughing like it was funny. His voice changed to the tone he used when he thought he could get his way with any girl he wanted.

I dashed into the forest toward the central aspen. A tree root caught my foot and I almost fell, but the forest lifted me up this time; it was helping me do this, giving me courage for what needed to be done.

"I'm waiting for you." My words were sweet.

He probably assumed that these were his trees, that this was his forest, and that I, by way of being on his property, was also his.

And that's why.

I let him catch me for a second. His hand was damp on my skin. He seemed thrilled, panting, hungry. "Gotcha!" he said. "Time to drink."

"You have to catch me first." I slipped away into the thicket and called him to follow again.

"Wait!" He must've felt lost, maybe afraid. Good. The forest didn't open up to strangers and he was an outsider. A stranger with a proposal to level the place. I whispered to the trees and the trees pulled Jackson in farther, blocked the place where he entered, closed around him like arms.

The oldest grove appeared empty from this direction, white and still. He wouldn't see the others surrounding the rocks and trees waking inside.

"There you are, Dhara. You're such a tease." He jumped over the rock wall, enthusiasm carrying him where he should never go.

When he was close, I grabbed his wrist and said, "Now, close your eyes. I have a surprise."

"I'm not sure I'm into this," he said.

"Promise." I leaned in and whispered into his ear, "It'll be worth it."

He closed his eyes and I led him inside, just beneath the largest tree of all. The trees ached and groaned. I sat him down on the ceremonial fabric that Will and Joce had covered in moss and bark.

"Keep them closed," I said.

"Okay, but this place creeps me out."

"How does this feel?" I tickled his arm with my fingernails and lifted a blade tucked beneath the edge of the fabric. Fast as fast, I slid it across his arm. The ground rumbled.

"Ouch! What the . . . ?" he yelped.

I let my lips graze his convincingly to take the pain away, then wiped his blood on the bark of the tree. It shuddered. I ran my hand against the largest of the sleeping trees. A bone stuck out of a branch, a knuckle or maybe a toe bone.

Joce and Will silently emerged from the shadows.

"Remember that night? At the beach? Do you remember what you did?" Joce said with Will.

"I'm sorry. I didn't mean anything by it."

I stroked his cheek.

"Dhara?" Branches latched tight around his wrists and

ankles. Roots crept around his legs and wound around his arms.

"Help me! Why aren't you helping me? This isn't funny, Dhara. I'm sorry! Okay?"

"Your father told us to keep silent. Big mistake."

The Children of the Aspen knew Mr. Tillman pressured me, said that if I told anyone what his son did, he'd have my family and everyone else kicked off our property. Our land that Jackson's father purchased at auction and was now renting back to us. Jackson had done this to other girls, so many others before. He'd bullied boys and hurt girls and now it was time for the forest to take him away.

He was alone in the center of the rock wall but watched as my kindred trees came to life. Shadows gathered inside. From my hands and feet roots grew and twisted around my friends, until they reached Jackson. The power I felt pour through me was immeasurable. The balance would be restored.

We all stayed strong and chanted together, "Feed the forest, right the wrongs." I knew it was the right thing to do even as his screams grew louder and the branches tangled between his teeth and twisted down his throat. The branches snaked up around his body inch by inch until he wasn't a boy anymore. He stopped struggling. Finally, it was done. All that was left was a tree the shape of a boy and a forest that was complete again. My friends hugged me, wiped my tears. My roots receded.

Will paused in front of the moaning trees and tossed Jackson's car's spark plugs into the forest as well, and the roots took them under the ground. As we walked through the forest, I turned back once to look at the others we'd brought to the forest a few years ago, the three who'd violated our open space. The only remnants of their bodies were a few finger bones protruding from a branch here and there. They were frozen in the bone forest forever.

Third Burn

by Courtney Gould

*T*HERE IS A SINGLE TREE STANDING IN THE AMBERVILLE CEMETERY.
Charlene Skaggit considers the ugly thing while she stands outside Kaitlyn Herring's house, the biting early-fall air seeping under her hoodie sleeves. Becca was only supposed to be saying a handful of goodbyes before they made for home, but it's been twenty minutes and here she is, annoyed and alone. It's certainly *one* way to spend her first night back on earth.

The night is only half-night, the sky still streaked with murky red from overbearing streetlights. The lights are off at Jay's Minimart, but across the street, the liquor store buzzes with life. Half of Main Street is dug up in a construction project that will probably take another decade to complete, if it's ever done. It's all gravel, harkening back to the olden days of wagons and horse-drawn buggies.

Charlie stares a little longer. She's not sure there were ever horse-drawn buggies here, actually.

Amberville, Oregon, is nowhere. A little bomb of life surrounded by a shockwave of dead and empty farmland, flat for as far as the eye can see. You can drive your haul out twenty minutes in any direction and it's still somebody's field. Is the owner still alive? Maybe. Has it been tended in a decade? Hard to say. What's supposed to be growing there? No one knows. North, there's wine country, which is the same thing, just add money. There are cities somewhere in the ether, too far to be convenient.

Anywhere you stand in Amberville, you can see the church. The very sturdy, very tall church that the rest of this town swirls around like planets in orbit. Red brick, white spire, cleaner than any other building for miles. In the dark, blocks away, you can't see the bare shrubs scorched down to their bones. You can't see the blackened dirt. You can't see the char marks on the foundation, though you can't see them in the daytime, either. City council has already had them painted over.

Charlie's stomach twists.

The screen door screeches at the front of the house and footsteps clap down the stairs and onto the grass, squelching with each step. Becca steps around the corner of the house, half-shrouded in night. Her curls still bounce, even after hours of socializing.

"Sorry about that," Becca says casually, tossing her hair over her shoulder. "Should we head out?"

"Let's roll."

It's been a strange night already—Charlie's first night out since going away. Her first time out with *Becca* since going away.

"Did you have fun?" Becca asks.

"Totally," Charlie muses. "Do you think everyone forgot about the summer?"

Becca doesn't laugh. Charlie clears her throat, and then it's quiet. Only the crunch of cars dipping from the main road to the gravel pit breaks the silence. They leave Kaitlyn's house together the way they did for years before the fire, but something's different now. Nights like this used to be the Becca and Charlie show, the two of them walking home with their shoulders knocking together, laughing until their fingers tangled and they found themselves holding hands.

Now Becca keeps a careful distance. She wraps her arms around herself to block out the cold as summer eases into a crisp fall, and it's like she's a thousand miles away. Like she's biding her time until this walk is over and she's free again.

Charlie bites the inside of her cheek. If she'd known this was how things would be, she wouldn't have done it. Whatever she thought would happen when she struck that match, watching the only relationship that matters burn to ashes wasn't worth it. It's not worth it to lose Becca.

It's not worth it to be alone.

At the end of Main Street, the road splits. One road leads to the nicer houses in Amberville, stacked high, painted white, with the warm glow of expensive light fixtures pouring onto the repaved street. On the other side is Charlie's house, a manufactured home one step above a trailer. Once upon a time, Charlie would walk Becca to her doorstep before ambling back down the road to her own less-than-beautiful home base. Tonight Becca pauses at the crossroad and faces Charlie.

"Well, this is where we split." She smiles but doesn't reach for a hug. "Good night."

"Night," Charlie says, and she wants to say more, but she can't find the words. She grinds the toe of her boot into a bit of loose asphalt on the road.

Before she can think of anything else to say, Becca turns and makes for home. Charlie watches her leave and she doesn't budge. She wants to grab Becca by the shoulders and ask her why it's different now, but she already knows the answer. Of course it's different when you take a match to the church, and of course it's different when you go away for five months to learn your lesson. But friendship is supposed to withstand something like this. She'd been dumb enough to think that, even if everything else were different when she came back, Becca would be the same.

But it was the opposite. Amberville is the same as it always was. Becca changed to match.

Charlie swallows hard and finds her way home in the dark. The screen door is ajar and the door behind it is unlocked. Her mother sleeps on the couch in their compressed living room, one leg dangling to the floor, mouth agape. The ashtray on the coffee table is littered with freshly spent cigarettes and the end table has a small collection of beer cans. The air is pungent and spicy with tobacco, a smell Charlie covers her nose to block out. Charlie picks up each one individually until she finds the one with a little beer left over. She tilts it to her lips and makes her way to her bedroom.

She opens the door but she doesn't turn on the light yet. Instead she downs the remainder of the beer.

When she lowers the can, she sees it.

For just a moment, a face on the far wall of her room. *Smiling.* Charlie blinks a few times, but it's not quite distinct enough to see clearly. Her blood runs cold as ice.

The smile widens.

Charlie flips on her bedroom light and there's no one. Nothing against the wall. Charlie's heart races, but there's nothing there. She forces herself to take one breath, then another. She returns her mother's now-empty beer can to its spot on the table and makes her way to bed, but when she closes her eyes, she still sees the face, lips tilting into an inhuman grin.

Just before she drifts away, she smells gasoline.

In the morning, Charlie runs.

She was never a fitness girl before the fire. But she doesn't run for the fitness; she runs to be alone. From the outside, Amberville looks shockingly small. Just a littering of squat buildings that trickle out to misaligned houses with neat, browning front lawns. She takes a left, another left, and then she's split from the town proper. The sidewalk meets a sudden end and then she's jogging in clumps of yellowed grass and gravel.

There's only one road out of Amberville, and the rest of the town is bordered by a thick, impenetrable wall of forest. Charlie runs all the way out to the trees before she slows down. The sun is bright and high, watery and cool. Charlie wipes a bit of sweat from her brow and closes her eyes.

When she opens her eyes, she feels even dizzier than when she started. There are a handful of benches on the trail at the forest edge. Since she can remember, Charlie has never seen a person *use* the path before, let alone one of the benches. But today a girl sits alone on the nearest bench. Her black hair is pulled neatly into a bun, legs crossed delicately, eyes facing Amberville with an expression Charlie can't quite decipher.

She turns to face Charlie with a suddenness that makes her jump.

"Morning," Charlie mutters, picking up the pace so she can sneak by.

The girl eyes her but doesn't say anything back. When Charlie gets close enough, the girl speaks. "Charlie Skaggit, right?"

Charlie pauses. Up close, the girl looks familiar, though she can't quite place her. Maybe someone from the party last night, though Charlie doubts it. She hardly paid attention to anyone at the party except Becca. There's a sharpness to this girl's face, though, cheeks angular and chin pointed. When Charlie looks at her, she smiles and it feels like sinking, like looking at the church spire all over again.

"That's me," Charlie says. "Why?"

"I'm new here," the girl says. "My name is Elle. I heard about you."

At that, Charlie rolls her eyes. *Heard about you,* as in *a friend of a friend of a friend told me what you did and now I want to see the criminal in person.* She shoves her fists into her hoodie pockets and says nothing.

"I'm sorry, that was abrupt," Elle says. Her words are just slightly stilted, like she's swallowing an accent. She dims her smile. "I really wanted to meet you. In person."

"Here I am," Charlie says. "Scared?"

"Why would I be scared?"

"I guess it depends on what you've heard."

The girl leans to the side to peer around Charlie, and then she smiles again. "I would be more scared if the church weren't still standing."

Charlie narrows her eyes. She's not sure what this girl is trying or what her aim is, but it feels different than the other kids in town. There are the ones who make fun of the whole thing and the ones who just ignore her like it'll make her go away. But this curiosity is new. This morbid fascination feels both invasive and comforting. Charlie shifts from one foot to the other.

"What do you want from me?" Charlie asks.

"Did you know this town burned down before?" Elle asks.

Charlie raises a brow.

"It's true. Twice, actually. Both over a hundred years ago. The whole town burned down to the bones and got built back up. Isn't that amazing?"

"Sure," Charlie murmurs. Because it's not amazing, it's annoying. Of course a town like Amberville would feel the need to rebuild a million times. "I wasn't trying to burn anything down. I just—"

"You weren't?" Elle cuts in. The look on her face is genuine surprise. "That's disappointing."

"What?"

Elle leans forward. Before Charlie has a chance to react, Elle takes her hand. The contact sends a cold spark up Charlie's arm. Her skin is cold, even colder than it should be in the crisp wind. A bit of her hair comes loose from her bun and it's like something shifts in her entire appearance. Suddenly a seed of fear takes root in Charlie's gut.

"I heard once that there is a curse on Amberville. They said it would burn three times to the ground and then it would never rise again. It's burned once, twice . . ." Elle licks her lips. "Amberville is ripe for it. One more time."

Charlie snatches her hand away. Without a word, she takes off running again, tennis shoes beating a pulse against the gravel, and she's not sure for a moment if she's running for her life. She thinks of the face on the wall last night. The eerie smile on Elle's face was too familiar, but there's no way. She's never seen this girl before. She couldn't have been in Charlie's room.

Something bubbles in Charlie's stomach and, before she has a chance to slow down and catch her breath, she buckles to her knees. Her fingers curl in the dead grass and she vomits. This isn't like drank-too-much sickness, though. Charlie looks down and the only thing she's vomited is water, clear and sparkling in the clumpy grass. Her eyes burn and her stomach rages, but it's only water.

She tastes the earthy tang of algae at the back of her throat and she vomits again. It keeps going, relentless, impossible for Charlie to catch her breath. The world begins to tilt around her, but for a moment Charlie looks over. Elle still sits on her bench wearing her unnerving smile. Like she knew this was coming.

Like she's glad.

"Tell me about classes," Mrs. Flores says without peeling her eyes from her notebook.

Charlie tilts her head and pops her neck. After spending years narrowly avoiding this room, she's finally face-to-face with the Amberville High School guidance counselor's office. The walls are plastered with motivational posters and infographics on college admissions, ways to beat anxiety, and numbers to call if it's starting to feel like it's not worth it to stick around. Mrs. Flores is a round woman with a particularly prominent mole on her upper lip and a half scowl that says she's got six other meetings to get through today.

But this was the compromise with the state. No juvenile detention if Charlie promised to meet with a guidance counselor every week to talk about her feelings.

"It's going fine," Charlie says. "My teachers won't make eye contact with me, but whatever."

"Which teachers?"

"All of them."

"Okay." Mrs. Flores finally looks up, and the bags under her eyes are even more prominent. "Try to think from their perspective. For a lot of us in town, our lives revolve around the church. It was very scary to think we might not have it anymore. Maybe some people are just trying to understand why you would put yourself in danger to destroy something so many people find joy in."

"But—"

"Let's really think about it from their point of view," Mrs. Flores persists. "What would you think of someone trying to take away something you love?"

Charlie doesn't speak. There's no point. The problem is right there in the question. *Think about it from* their *point of view.* Charlie wonders if Mrs. Flores even realizes the difference between saying *their* point of view and *our* point of view. Charlie doesn't need to imagine this town taking away something she loves because it already has. Between an alcoholic mother and a father who's been missing since conception, what Amberville took away is greater than a church. It's a future.

"You don't want to talk about classes. That's fine," Mrs. Flores says. She puts her pencil down and rests her chin in her palm. "Let's talk about what happened before. As you know, everything you say to me is in confidence. How about you tell me what was going through your head."

"I don't know," Charlie says.

It's not a lie. Not exactly.

It was a warm night when it happened, spring stretching long into summer. Unlike most days, Charlie hadn't gone home after school. Instead, she'd gone to Becca's house for the first time. And it was like stepping into a new world—not just lavish furniture, but speckled ceramic pans, shoe racks, curtains on tall windows. Becca's house was made of little details Charlie couldn't begin to imagine in her own house. It was like, for a single night, slipping out of the world of *them* and pretending it was *us*. Just once, she could see the life that the rest of Amberville was living.

She ate cornbread and roasted vegetable soup for dinner and Becca talked with her father about her classes for the day and Charlie watched them, wistful. One day this would be her life too.

Becca whispered something to her father, and then they both turned.

"Charlie," Becca's father had said. "Will you come to church with us this Sunday?"

The Amberville church was, as Charlie's mother described it, foreign ground. Where almost everyone else in town went every Sunday like clockwork, Charlie had never stepped foot inside. Of course there were no tickets to church, no admission fees, but it still felt like an exclusive club she didn't belong to.

But here it was, arms open wide, waiting for her.

So she agreed to go. And that's when the problem started.

While Charlie helped Becca with the dishes, she heard the whispering. Becca's parents in the hallway, her mother hissing that they couldn't bring Charlie to church. That she'd already made the house smell like cigarettes. *It's already bad enough she's here*, she'd whispered. *I counted my dishes before dinner just in case any go missing.*

If Becca heard her parents, she didn't show it. But Charlie heard every word, punctures like snake's venom. It was astounding how quickly she could go from the top of the world to rock bottom. She pressed her nose to the flap of her hoodie and, of course, Becca's mother was right. She smelled like home, looked like home, probably acted like it too. Tobacco and musk and filth. As much as she liked to fantasize about being the exact perfect girl Amberville wanted, it wasn't possible.

This would never be her life.

Without giving even a warning, Charlie had slipped out of Becca's house that night and made her way to the one place she would never belong. The church was beautifully manicured then, washed bricks stacked neatly with ivy climbing the sides of its arched entrance.

She could come here if she wanted, sure. She could sit in the back pew all alone, listening to sermons she didn't understand. Even then, she wouldn't belong. Even then, the others would see her and think of the smell, the baggy clothes, the ticking clock until she proved herself to be the trash they already believed she was.

There was a buzzing in her ears that night, a movement to the wind like a hand guiding her. She didn't know where the match came from. But when it appeared in her hand, she knew what she was meant to do with it.

And even if it failed, that initial spark was enough.

Charlie blinks, slowly floating back to reality. Mrs. Flores is eyeing her cautiously, lips pursed. Sunlight trickles in through the window and the memory flutters away.

"Can I ask you a question?"

"Of course."

"I heard that Amberville burned down before. Completely. Twice."

Mrs. Flores leans back in her chair. "Is that why you did it? You wanted to be the third girl to burn it down?"

So Elle wasn't lying. "I didn't know. Can you tell me?"

Reluctantly, Mrs. Flores clears her throat apparently just glad to get a conversation going. "Okay . . . yes, we can talk about it. There is a little folk tale here in Amberville from back when the town was founded. Apparently, there was a young girl practicing witchcraft in town, and it caused all kinds of problems. Drought, fires, sick cattle. The legend says that, to stop it all, they burned the girl at the stake right outside the Amberville Christian Church. And before she died, she told the town that it would burn three times to the ground and then—"

"—it would never rise again," Charlie finishes.

Mrs. Flores eyes her skeptically. "You *do* know the story."

"I only heard it recently."

If Mrs. Flores says something else, Charlie doesn't hear it. The room falls silent like they've been plunged underwater, ears full and head buzzing. Mrs. Flores's mouth closes and her stare is wide-eyed and unblinking.

"Mrs. Flores?" Charlie croaks.

Mrs. Flores reaches across the desk and grabs Charlie by her thick red curls. She slams her face into the desk hard enough to bruise. Charlie scrambles against her grip, but it's useless. She's slammed against the wood again, then again. She gasps at the suddenness of it. At the violence. Somewhere behind her, she hears shouting. *Cheering.* When she gasps for air, the room snaps back to reality.

"... and then in the 1870s, another young girl apparently felt the need to burn it down all over again."

Mrs. Flores is rambling now, and probably has been the whole time. But Charlie's nerves are on fire. She touches her cheek where it hit the desk, but there's no soreness, no blood. She breathes hard, brain frantic. She needs to get out of here. Fast.

"If you ask me, every town has fires. I don't think that two fires necessarily means that—"

"I have to go," Charlie says. "I'm sorry."

Mrs. Flores glances at her wall clock. "Okay. It's just about time anyway. But next week we're going to do some actual work."

Charlie nods and throws open the office door, tumbling into the hallway toward daylight. She leans against a locker and catches her breath. Her pulse thrums behind her eyes and she tries not to panic. Something is happening to her. Something is happening to Amberville.

"Charlie?"

Charlie opens her eyes and Becca stands in front of her, brows raised in concern. Charlie wipes the sweat from her brow and smiles. "Hey."

"Are you okay?" Becca asks.

"I'm okay. Just kind of . . . going through it." She swallows and rights herself, straightening out her hoodie. "Are you ready?"

Becca shifts from one foot to the other, eyes glued to the hallway tile. Her hands are shoved into her pockets while she chews on her words like she always does before eventually spitting them out. Finally she says, "Can we talk first?"

"What's wrong?"

"You heard about the gym today?" Becca asks. "All the stuff they found?"

"No," Charlie says. "What did they find?"

"Gasoline." Becca waits for a reaction, but Charlie doesn't offer one. "Like, barrels of gasoline in the upper gym. Just in the middle of the basketball court."

"Okay?"

"I guess they're gonna start investigating who put it there."

"I hope they find out," Charlie says. Heat flushes in her cheeks. "Are you ready to go now?"

"You don't know anything about it?"

"No, I don't."

"Okay."

Becca doesn't move. Students keep filtering out of the hall, making their way to the two main exits, but Becca stays completely still. She doesn't make eye contact, eyeing the floor instead. Charlie waits for her to say something, but she doesn't.

She's never had a hard time interpreting Becca's expression before, but right now she's lost.

"Do *you* think I know something?"

"It's just that it feels like something you'd . . . After the stuff with the church," Becca says, barely able to string together a coherent sentence. "Some people are saying that you'd only use that much if you were gonna—"

"—start a fire," Charlie nearly spits out. "Well, it wasn't me."

Becca keeps staring at the floor.

"Jesus." Charlie adjusts her grip on her backpack straps, palms sweating. "I'm not going to. I'm *not*. Can you just believe me?"

"What am I supposed to do?" Becca asks. "I wish you'd just tell me. I know you have, like . . . mental issues."

And it's like the floor comes out from under her. Of course she'd known for a while that Becca's mind had changed. Now that she'd come back from community service, she had no friends. But to hear it so plain hurts worse than the slam against the desk. Worse than the retching. She's never been so completely alone.

"Never mind," Charlie says.

"Charlie—"

"I'm leaving."

When she gets home, there are no cars in the driveway. Charlie slams through the front door, letting the screen scream shut behind her. She throws her backpack at the sofa and crashes into her room, sucking in one deep breath and then another to keep from crying.

Something moves in the doorway behind her.

Elle stands, leaning against the door, watching Charlie's melt-down like it's daytime TV. Charlie grabs Elle by the arm and tugs her into the room, shutting the door behind her. She doesn't know what she means to say yet, but the anger boils up in her, hot at the base of her throat. For a brief moment Elle looks surprised. They're left in the cool, empty quiet, Charlie breathing hot in Elle's face.

"Who *are* you?" she demands.

Elle smiles in that same eerie way, forcing Charlie to release her. Her shoulders are relaxed, stance easy. She's not concerned about this confrontation at all. She's only amused by it. She brushes her hair over her shoulder and folds her arms. "What do you think, Charlene?"

"What do I think?"

"I don't care what anyone else thinks," Elle muses. "Only you."

Charlie stamps down the way those words stir something in her. Outside the window, other kids are getting home from school, backpacks slung over their shoulders, chattering carelessly to each other. They aren't alone in here discovering . . . *whatever* she's discovered.

"What do you think?" Elle says again, but her voice is different. Her face is different, skin pale and tight like porcelain. She asks, but it's not a question. It's a command.

"I don't know what you are."

Elle looks out the window, but Charlie can't tell what she looks *at*. After a moment her lips curl into a smile. "Have you seen something frightening? Something only you could see?"

Charlie swallows. "Are you a witch?"

"I *was* a witch. They weren't wrong." Elle's fingertips twitch at her sides now. "I still am, I suppose. My friends and I held hands in the trees, danced naked, waited for the Devil at the stroke of midnight. We loved each other more than we loved this ugly little town. We wanted to be part of something *bigger*."

Charlie's chest aches. There's a familiarity to her words even now. Familiarity like a sinkhole. It would be a miserable thing to live in this one place forever, talk to only these people, die having seen only these hills.

"They came for me at midnight. My mother let them into the house so it would be quiet. I didn't have a chance to run. They took me by the wrists and ankles. The people who were supposed to love me," Elle says without even a hint of sadness. "They all stared at me. They waited for me to die. They *wanted* me to die."

"I'm sorry," Charlie breathes.

"I don't know if it was me who said it or if it was the Devil. The curse. But when I said it, I knew it would be true. I didn't know how to stop it."

"Did you want to?"

Elle considers. "No."

"I'm not a witch," Charlie says. "I don't even know how I'd—"

"I don't want you to become a witch. I would never ask that." Elle settles into the chair opposite Charlie. Carefully, cautiously, she slides a hand over Charlie's knuckles and leans close. The slight pout of her lower lip is all Charlie can see. "That's the crux of it, Charlene. I am not the one asking you to change who you are. Who is trying to change you?"

Charlie glances out the window. She doesn't mean to, but it's involuntary. Elle follows her gaze to Becca, innocently walking her dog outside. Becca with her cozy sweater and scarf and little white dog, bouncing along like she's not afraid of being seen. Like being perceived isn't a nightmare. Like their fight earlier didn't implode her world. She is so easily what Amberville wants her to be. Reshaping herself doesn't feel like carving away her skin and bone. It doesn't hurt her the way it hurts Charlie. It isn't fair.

"What do they whisper about her when she isn't there?" Elle asks, her voice only a breath. *"What a good girl. Her mother must be so proud."*

Charlie winces.

"What do they say about you?"

Charlie turns. Elle is shockingly close to her now. Her breath presses hot against Charlie's neck. Their knees touch, Elle's elbow against Charlie's, and Charlie feels each point of contact like it burns. Elle may not really be here, may be just a figment of her imagination, but *this* is real. It is searingly, frighteningly real. Charlie's heart races, but she doesn't lean away. She holds still, even as the goose bumps prick their way up her arms.

"I don't understand."

"In a perfect world, the people in this town would love you for what you are," Elle says. "But they don't. Centuries have passed. They haven't learned. Three chances to get better and they refuse. What else are we meant to do?"

"*We?*" Charlie asks.

Elle smiles. "You tried to continue a legacy you didn't even know about. Who better to be the last one? The final one."

Charlie shakes her head. "I can't do it."

"What would it change?" Elle asks. "That last attempt was just proof that this town added to a case they've been making against you since you were born. You're not the first person to suffer like this. You've already met the others."

"Others?"

"The first two girls to take a stand. Naomi, who was shunned for living alone and refusing motherhood. After she set the town ablaze, they stuck her head underwater until she drowned. Iris, who was punished for loving another woman, beaten to death after she struck the match."

The river water vomit, the vision she had of Mrs. Flores. It makes sense now, and it overwhelms her. There is something so much bigger than she imagined happening here. A legacy only inches from the finish line and Charlie is holding the baton. She looks at Elle, and Elle nods.

"If I do it, will I die, too?" Charlie asks.

"Maybe," Elle says. "But I can help you. I've already started."

"Where would I go?"

"There's a place for girls like you, Charlene Skaggit. There's a place in the woods. A home for girls without a home. Would you like to find a place you fit?"

Charlie nods.

When Charlene Skaggit wakes from her sleep, she is not alone.

The air is heavy in her bedroom. It sits on her chest like a stone, pressing her hard into her mattress. She gasps for air and the room echoes back to her, empty and full all at once. She doesn't need anyone to tell her it's time. Her bones sing with fear and anticipation all at once. It's too quiet, but her thoughts are loud enough to drown it all away.

She shifts a little in her bed and feels it there, tucked into her sweaty palm. A single match, tip coarse against her calloused skin.

"Elle?" Charlie asks, but the room is empty. The window is open, and her sheer curtains flutter in the breeze. It's quieter than silence should be, sound turned in on itself. It's like she's reached the peak of a mountain, like her ears are full of cotton. The pressure in the air is so heavy, it's like a second skin. Her voice sounds far away, in another room, in another life.

She doesn't need to look for Elle. Her fingertips ghost the curve of her collarbone and she knows. It's not that there's someone else in the room. Elle is with her now in a way she can't see. Elle is with her in the way her feet gracefully meet the wood floor and the breeze skirts her hair over her shoulders. She looks in the mirror and she sees Elle in the brightness of her eyes and the curious quirk of her brow. It's a heavy thing, to have another person swelling in the empty chamber of her chest. The stories always said that Amberville's first witch danced with the Devil. Maybe it's true, maybe it isn't, but one thing is certain.

The Devil is in her room tonight.

Charlie stands in her dark room and stares at the mirror a moment longer. She waits for her expression to match the one she's used to, but it's like looking into a face she doesn't know. A face that isn't her own.

"What do I do?" Charlie asks.

There is no voice to answer her, but she knows. She pulls on a pair of running shorts and a tank top, massages her curls into a massive ponytail. Her heart races, but her mind is oddly calm. There is comfort in knowing you're only a piece of a larger machine, she realizes now. In knowing that you are only one line in a saga, and that this night would always come. Since over a century ago, with a curse screamed into the black night, this moment was always coming. Charlie would always wake up at midnight with the Devil's hand on her shoulder. She would always find a match in her palm.

She makes her way out of the house and the night is too quiet.

In the dark, the scent of gasoline opens on her tongue like a blossom. The drums of gasoline found in the gym, she assumes, spilled across town in preparation. Maybe Becca was right the whole time, but it doesn't matter anymore. There's something happening now, rolling forward fast and hard and beyond stopping. It's not about the memories made in this place, about the friends clawing their way to an escape. It's not about the farmers expanding acre by acre away from this rotting heart. It's not about the girls this place sacrificed to stay alive. It's not about any one thing; it's about all of it.

Charlie balances carefully on a thick root at the Amberville Cemetery tree and she feels it. Elle's blood runs in her veins, builds up in the empty cavity of her chest like the swelling of a symphony. There is a world beyond Amberville, and it's arms are open wide.

But only if Amberville burns.

From the tree, she sees it all. The empty farmland, the bruised vineyards, the forest pressing in. Elle tried, and Naomi tried, and Iris tried. But a curse is a curse, and Amberville sprouted up from the ashes over and over, learning nothing, always just as stuck as before. A legacy is what it is because it never ends, right? But Amberville could end. All the pain doesn't have to be for nothing.

There's a place for girls like you, Charlene Skaggit, the wind breathes. It's soft against Charlie's neck. She leans into the gentle touch, fingers fluttering at her sides. She hasn't struck the match yet, but it burns hot in her grip. *There's a place in the woods. A home for girls without a home.*

Charlie closes her eyes. In one motion, gentler than she's ever been, she slides the match against the bark of the tree, feels the flame spark to life against her skin. The third burning of Amberville is within reach. She could be the bringer of the end.

It could end tonight.

After a lifetime of wishing she could fit in the rigid grooves of this place, she understands it all. Every girl lost to the crumbling passage of time, every girl who ran from this place, every girl punished by its ire, they all stand at her side now, hands joined with hers. Their whispers meet her in the shape of a cool breeze. She isn't alone. She never was.

Drop it, Charlene.

The voice isn't on the breeze, Charlie realizes. It echoes in her own skull. It's Elle, still with her, voice sweet like honey.

Drop it and run to me.

Charlie Skaggit sucks in a breath and eyes the dark trees on the horizon. They sway tenderly in the night wind. She feels the tree behind her—once a pyre, a killing thing—the rough fiber of it under her fingers. The single flame on the matchstick burns closer now, licking her knuckles. There's a place in the trees. There's a place for her. Belonging is not a thing that's given; it has to be taken by force.

She drops the match and runs.

It Stays with You

by Aden Polydoros

IT WAS SUPPOSED TO BE THE BEST SUMMER OF OUR LIVES—THAT ONE final send-off before Quinn and Sarah went to college upstate, and the cancer finished gnawing on Gabe's lungs and moved on to his brain, and I got left behind in this backwater shithole of a town I'd probably die in. But that was before the party. Before the mirror.

We were in Quinn's house, one of those nice Spanish-style homes in the center of town. A cookie-cutter house in a cookie-cutter neighborhood, and part of me hated him for it. He was the kind of guy you knew would end up with a high school sweetheart, office job, and three kids, and I resented him for that, too. As for the dare, I was so far down the bottle that I couldn't remember who had suggested it, only that I laughed and took another swig of the Smirnoff we'd been passing around. The label said it was sorbet-flavored, but the aftertaste of cotton candy lingered in the back of my throat with each sip, sickly sweet and rancid.

"You can't be serious," I said, passing the bottle off to Sarah. The edges of the room were pleasantly blurred, and a dopey warmth radiated from my chest downward. Along with the vodka, and the beer before that, I'd had half of Gabe's weed brownie. "Bloody Mary? I mean, seriously. The last time we tried that, we were—what? Ten? I remember, we chickened out after saying her name just once."

I looked at Quinn as I said it. I wanted to remind him that he hadn't been there. That this might've been his house, but he was just a visitor here.

He challenged me with a smarmy smirk. "I'll bet you were the one who wimped out, huh, Marlow? I mean, hate to break it to you, bro, but you've always been a bit of a scaredy-cat. Remember that time in third grade?"

"The firefighters!" Sarah exclaimed, pointing the vodka bottle at me like a baton.

I shot her a disgruntled look. "That was different."

"I remember now," she said with a laugh. "You wouldn't even go over to their truck. You hid in the janitor's closet and nearly gave Mrs. Greenwich a heart attack."

"Yeah, well, fire trucks are stupid." My cheeks burned.

"Come on, Marlow," Gabe teased. "What's a measly little mirror got on a fire truck?"

Rolling my eyes, I pushed him gently in the shoulder, careful, the way you eased a dog away from the table. Through his T-shirt, my fingers traced over the hard ridge of his bone. There wasn't much flesh left on him anymore, just taut skin that the TV's glow blanched to a cadaverous green.

"I think it'll be fun," Sarah said, passing the bottle to Quinn without drinking from it.

Quinn lifted the bottle, his throat pulsating as he took a long slug. His shirt collar slipped, and I caught a glimpse of it only for a moment—that webby pink patch of scar tissue stretching down his chest. See, before he fell in with us last summer, he'd been with the popular crowd. At some beach party or another, some idiot had spritzed lighter fluid onto a bonfire, or maybe it was a firecracker tossed onto the embers. In any case, Quinn got burned. Bad. He couldn't toss a football after that, and by the time he healed, his group had moved on.

Anyway, in my mind, Quinn was still the same jock who'd given me crap up through sophomore year, and now he'd become the fourth wheel to our middle-school trio, when we'd always worked better as a tricycle sort of squad. But Sarah liked him, and I loved Sarah like a sister. Which was why when Quinn got on my nerves, I kept my mouth shut.

Sarah looked around and said, "Where should we do it?

Where's a mirror?"

"I still think this is ridiculous," I said, but my voice felt small compared to the others', as if I were already fading into the background.

Quinn lowered the bottle, wiping his mouth with the back of his hand. "The master bathroom has a floor-to-ceiling mirror."

"Who'll go first?" Sarah asked.

A silence fell over us. Even Quinn, who had seemed so eager to play, now restlessly drummed his fingers against his leg. Somehow, in the carnival glow of his dad's vintage jukebox and the Technicolor pulse of the TV, all our childish superstitions seemed to rear their ugly heads.

"I volunteer as tribute," Gabe said, and I rolled my eyes.

"You go do that, Katniss," I said.

He climbed to his feet and gave a flourish of a bow. I rose as well, grasping onto the sofa arm to stabilize myself. He might've been the one with cancer, but I felt as if I'd hit my own dead end. The truth was, I couldn't see myself living beyond twenty-five, or thirty maybe. Figured one day I'd blow my brains out or make a sharp turn on the I-75, plow right into a cement wall. It wasn't a plan yet, not really, just a deep and gnawing wish that I could disappear with no one knowing and no body to leave behind.

We followed Gabe into the master bedroom. Through the floorboards, the thrum of the jukebox vibrated in low, palpitating tremors, the voices muffled as though prematurely buried.

As we reached the bathroom, Gabe hesitated. I could see it in his eyes—he didn't want to go in alone. Call it juvenile superstition. That was what I thought at the time, except now I wonder if it was intuition.

"I think we have to do it together," he said at last, looking around the circle. "Right? Isn't that how it works?"

For a long, unwavering moment, there was only silence and the beat of my own heart. The world swam and trembled in the dim pinkish light. I closed my eyes to catch a break, bothered by the glow of the pendant lamp overhead.

"Yeah, I guess," Sarah said, so we clambered into the bathroom, squeezing in so that all of us could fit in front of the mirror. Gabe sidled in front of me, his gaunt form folding into mine, the sharp end of his elbow resting like an anvil against my stomach.

Our closeness awoke something in me, but I didn't know how to put it in words. Just that I wished he could grow onto me like cancer. I drained the rest of the Smirnoff and set the bottle on top of the sink, where it wouldn't be knocked over by straying hands.

"The lights," Sara said, and Quinn fumbled with them before engulfing us in the dark. Maybe it was the booze, or Gabe's closeness, but with the lights out, the room didn't feel so tight. I got a weird feeling the walls were rotating like a fun-house ride, and reached out just to see if they'd shift. No. Still and steady.

"Do we all say it," I asked, "or just one each?"

"I think we all say it," Quinn said.

"On the count of three, then," Sarah said.

One. Two. Three. The skin prickled on my nape, like there was something breathing down the back of my neck.

"Bloody Mary," we said in unison. We waited for a moment, with the sort of fumbling, awkward unease of a first kiss, before trying again. "Bloody Mary."

Sarah gasped.

"What is it?" Gabe asked, his voice rising in alarm.

"Quinn, was that you?" she asked, before swatting his arm.

"Hey, what was that for?" he asked, rubbing his shoulder.

"I know you just pinched me," she said.

"I didn't. I swear."

"You're such a jerk. That really hurt."

I rolled my eyes. "Let's just continue and get this over with."

"One more time," Gabe said, but even he sounded a bit uneasy, and when my palm brushed against his, his fingers were clammy.

I wanted to pretend we were kids again, swapping scary stories in his bedroom or hunting for geckos and anoles in Sarah's backyard. Before I was seven, fear had never felt so close, and with each year it only drew closer, like a panther circling in.

We counted down the final time, and I stared at my own faint reflection in the mirror. In the gloom, my features appeared to shift and meld, my nose and eyes flowing together and re-forming into something stranger. Just an optical illusion, or maybe that weed brownie had been danker than I thought.

For the third and final time, we whispered, "Bloody Mary."

Seconds later, Quinn started screaming.

"What's going on?" Gabe shouted.

I twisted around, knocked into someone. An elbow jabbed me in the ribs. "Christ, Sarah, turn on the lights!"

Swearing, Sarah fumbled for the switch. In the corner of my eye, I glimpsed a figure in the mirror—a man with a fox's crafty smile and a trucker's tugged-down cap. My breath seized in my throat, my stomach plummeting like a sack of lead shot. But then the lights flashed on, and the only thing to confront me was my own pale, quivering reflection.

"I'm burning," Quinn shrieked, writhing on the floor. His hands curled over his face, nails digging into his scalp. "Put it out. Oh God, please, someone put it out."

Quinn's eyes met mine through the net of brown hair cast over his brow. He groaned, his lips peeling back to reveal teeth stained bright red, like he'd been eating a candy apple. More blood inched from his nose, drawing a crimson trail down his chin. As the first droplets plopped onto the daisy-patterned shower mat, the convulsions began.

They called it a brain aneurysm, just a vessel in Quinn's head that had sprung a leak at the perfect moment, flooding all his brain's twisted little passageways with blood until it gushed from his ears and nose. An aneurysm. While we were waiting for an ambulance, he died with his head resting in Sarah's lap.

There was a funeral at least, one with an open casket. The mortician had cleaned all the blood up and slapped some blush onto his cheeks, and when I came up with my mom, she whispered how he looked just like he was sleeping. Except that was bullshit, because he looked like he was dead.

When I turned around to make my way back to my seat, a man in the last row caught my eye. Reddish-blond stubble darkened his cheeks, and his lips were so cracked that threads of blood welled from the creases when he smiled at me. Underneath the sweat-yellowed brim of his trucker's cap, his blue eyes met mine, their whites red and swollen, as if he'd been weeping.

My legs locked in place. Faint noises filtered down to me—the merry twinkle of carnival tunes, the rattle and clunk of roller-coaster cars plowing down a track, a wet doglike panting.

Staring me straight in the eye, he lifted his right hand and touched his raised index finger to his lips.

Fingers tightened around my shoulder. "Marlow?"

I flinched, wrenching away with a low moan. My shoulders loosened. It was just my mom, peering over at me with her brow furrowed.

"Is something wrong?" she asked softly. Yeah, that was the million-dollar question, wasn't it? I'd been waiting years for her to ask me it, except not for what she thought, because *she didn't even fucking know.*

And she'd never know, if I could keep it that way. I'd die before I told her. My skin crawled just from the thought of it, because if she found out somehow, it would ruin me in her eyes. She'd never look at me the same way again. And worse—she'd blame me. Or she'd blame herself. Or maybe she'd just tell me it was nothing at all, that it happened to everyone, that I was being too sensitive, and it'd already been ten years, so why the fuck couldn't I just get over it?

"It's nothing," I said, feeling like a coward and hating myself for it. When I turned back, the man was gone.

It wasn't the first time I had imagined him in a crowd, and I knew in my heart it wouldn't be the last.

Later that afternoon, over sweet tea and stale doughnuts at Quinn's house, I found myself alone on the patio.

"I thought it'd be me," Gabe said from behind me.

I didn't look back. His shadow fell over my Styrofoam cup and half-eaten powdered doughnut. I took another sip to keep my hands busy and my mouth full. Dead leaves and gardenia petals floated in the pool, and I tried not to look at the water for too long—there was something wrong about the sky's reflection and the loquat trees' proportions.

"I thought I'd be the first to die, I mean," he said, sinking into the seat next to me. The seat's interwoven rubber strips groaned beneath him, and the entire chair shuddered.

We'd talked about death before, and I wanted to keep this conversation in line with the others—holding it at a distance, not close enough for it to bite.

"You kidding, Gabe?" I kept my voice lighthearted, or at least tried to. "You're gonna outlive us all. Cockroaches never die."

He rolled his eyes, reaching over to steal the second half of my doughnut. He only took a bite, not like he'd have done in the old days, with a better appetite. "Lately I feel more like a radioactive spider."

"Better not bite me then."

As Sarah came up, our uneasy banter faded into silence. Normally, having her here would make me feel better, but today it felt dangerous. As if just by being together, we were summoning something. Without a word, she took the chair across from us. The fourth remained pushed out, like an absence.

"The mirror," she said, and I exhaled slowly.

"It was just a coincidence, Sarah. I mean, Bloody Mary?" I trailed off as her deep brown eyes met mine. All I could think about was the night Quinn died, how with a final convulsion, he'd coughed hard enough to fan blood across her cheeks.

"I saw something," Gabe said suddenly.

I turned, looking at him helplessly. Come on, he was just going to leave me here alone?

"It was my own reflection, but . . ." He moistened his lips, his fingers straying to his face. He traced the hard ridge of his cheek-bone, following it to where his teeth lay beneath his skin. When he pressed down, I could almost see their outlines. "Worse."

"Worse how?" Sarah asked.

I groaned. "Oh, come on."

"Thinner," Gabe said softly.

When I swallowed, my throat clicked. I searched desperately for something to say, anything, except condolences had never come easily to me. All I could think was how I once thought he was so handsome, but with each week, he'd whittle down into more and more of a stranger. Someday, I might not even recognize him.

"Gabe, it wasn't real," I said, taking a hasty sip of sweet tea so I had time to think between words. "It was just, you know . . . It was just a trick of the light."

I had seen him under different lighting before—the sunlight, the stadium lamps, those dark, intimate spaces beneath the bleachers where only shafts of moonlight and the glow of a shared joint could reach—and I knew the way that shadow and light could transform him, his cheeks hollowed out, his face like a skull becoming.

"Marlow, I saw something too," Sarah said, looking from Gabe to me.

"Yeah, and what'd you see?" I took my doughnut from Gabe's hand and tore off a chunk, chewed, grimaced. The powder coated my tongue, first sweet, but then as dry and sour as mildew.

"These doughnuts taste like ass."

Sarah's expression remained serious. "My stepdad."

Gabe drew in a sharp breath, and the doughnut gummed in my throat, sealing it tight. I stared at her, and she stared back.

Yeah. Her stepdad. She'd told us about him before, a little bit at a time over the years, in broken pieces, like spitting out busted teeth. The beltings, the pinching, the shouting. He'd fed her dog food when she was five, and she'd never forget choking down those wet, gelatinous chunks. Back in eighth grade, Gabe and I had made a secret promise that if he ever came down from Kentucky, we'd take a bat to his head. Now that Gabe was dying, I guessed maybe I'd have to do it alone someday.

"What you probably saw was my ugly face," I said, but Sarah didn't even crack a smile.

"I know what I saw, Marlow. And I know you saw something too."

"I didn't see shit."

Her dark eyes riveted me to my seat. "You saw something."

Fat popped and sizzled on the grill's hot grate. Flames licked the steaks' marbled edges, and crimson juices gushed down the sides of the raw cuts.

"Mom told me what happened to your friend," Brock said,

glancing over at me as he flipped a rib eye. With his dress shirt's sleeves rolled up, and his hair slicked back so that only a few artful curls framed his brow, he looked like he was attempting to re-create an Abercrombie ad. Even now he couldn't help but find a way to rub his success in my face—first in his class at Warrington, with a wedding ring glinting on his finger, and the top-dog asshole attitude of a crypto bro.

He was the star of the family. He could never do wrong. God, I hated his guts.

"Must be awful to die like that," Brock continued when I didn't answer.

Turning away from the grill, I glanced down at a dead moth on the patio pavers. Ants swarmed its body, gnawing at its abdomen. Back inside, Brock's daughter, Emma, giggled at something on the TV. The cartoon voices sounded weird from out here, like they were blathering in another language.

Technically, I was Emma's uncle; only, it didn't feel that way. Even though I was going to be eighteen this October, I still felt scared like a kid inside. Mom kept asking me what I wanted to do with my future, but the truth was that it was hard to see beyond the next few months, much less the next year.

"I heard it happened so fast, Quinn never felt a thing." I shifted on the sun lounger. Overhead, dark mildew stained the porch slats like dried blood splatter.

"You sure you're all right?" Brock asked.

"He used to bully me, you know."

"Your friend?"

"Back in tenth grade," I said. "Back when he was still one of the popular kids. I never forgot that."

"Oh." Brock turned his attention back to the grill.

"Hey, Brock, you ever play Bloody Mary?"

"No, I'm not a big fan of children's games," he said, glancing back at me.

"Yeah, I figured."

"Heard that's what you guys were doing that night, huh?"

"Yeah."

"Were you smoking anything?"

I rolled my eyes. He asked it so casually, but I could tell from the way he looked at me, he'd narc to Mom in an instant.

"We just had a couple beers." I glanced down as my phone vibrated.

Gabe had left a single text message: **can we talk?**

"Yeah, right," Brock said. "Really, what'd you have?"

Ignoring him, I pushed the call button and rose to my feet. I stepped back inside, not wanting Brock to eavesdrop on me when it already felt like he'd gotten his head crammed halfway up my ass. Like he and Emma just so happened to "drop by" the same afternoon as Quinn's funeral. He said it was because Emma had a casting call down in Miami on Saturday, and this was just a one-night pit stop on the way, but I didn't buy it. If he wanted to get me to talk, he'd have to ply me with something a whole lot better than clearance rib eyes.

As the phone rang, I made my way to my bedroom. The door hung ajar.

"Marlow?" Gabe asked, his voice just a static-slurred whisper. "Hey, Marlow? You there?"

I eased open my door and stepped inside. With mounds of dirty clothing on the floor and dishes stacked on the dresser and nightstand, Mom always joked how it looked as if a small tornado had passed through. There was no one in the bedroom, but my bathroom door was open, and the faucet was running. I swallowed hard, my mouth suddenly dry. A square of light shone through the opening.

"Trucks?" Emma asked, giggling. "You're so silly."

My stomach felt stretched between a pair of ice-cold hands, wrung into a sopping mess. As I stepped into the bathroom, I held my breath. It felt safer that way.

Emma leaned over the sink, her eyes planted on the mirror and the stupidest smile slapped across her lips. When I touched her shoulder, she looked up.

"Hey, Marly," she said.

"What do you think you're doing?" An uncontrollable tremor warbled my words.

She cocked her head. "I was talking to the funny man."

I swiveled around to face the mirror. My own reflection stared back at me through a film of steam—blue eyes dazed like a deer in headlights, mouth quivering. Quickly, I turned back to her.

"The funny man?" I asked. "Who's the funny man?"

"The man in the mirror." Her smile only grew, as if she were in on all this. Some big joke. "He asked me if I like trucks. Isn't that a silly question?"

The phone slipped from my hand and landed on the terry cloth shower mat. I gripped her shoulders without thinking.

"Listen to me, Emma, don't ever talk to him again, you hear? Don't you even look at him. If he comes, you run and hide!"

Tears rose in her eyes in an instant. Frightened by my voice, or the fear I struggled to contain, or something else entirely, she burst into frantic sobs. Alerted by the commotion, Brock and Mom rushed into the bedroom.

"What the hell is going on?" Brock demanded as he scooped Emma into his arms.

"Daddy, I didn't do anything," Emma blubbered, burying her head in his shoulder. "Marly just started yelling at me."

I swiveled around. "Mom, why'd you let her in my room?"

"Christ, Marlow! She was just using the bathroom. The other one is clogged."

"You shouldn't have done that," I said, my voice rising in near hysteria. "Don't let her in here again."

Brock and our mom exchanged a knowing look. He handed Emma off to Mom, who stroked the girl's hair and carried her back through the bedroom door.

"Come on, sweetie," my mom said. "Let's see if the pie is ready."

Once they were out of sight, Brock turned back to me. Stepping forward, he fisted his hands at his sides.

"The hell is wrong with you?" he growled.

I swallowed. "Brock."

"You want to know something, Marly? Want to know why we're here?"

"Don't call me that."

"It's because Mom's worried about you."

I scoffed. "Since when did you ever care about me, Brock? You've always hated me. You thought I was a nuisance. I know you did—"

"Whatever happened to you? You used to be a good kid." He shook his head in disgust. "What is it? Drugs? You on something? Is that it?"

He kept on ranting, but my gaze had already drifted away. The water had started to overflow from the sink, and steam clouded the mirror like a cataract-filmed eye.

A handprint was outlined in the haze as if a man had pressed his palm against the other side of the glass. As I watched, the shapes of fingers dissolved from sight.

That night, for the first time, I took Gabe with me to the truck stop just outside of town, a cracked slab of asphalt that appeared on the verge of sinking into the cypress swamp bordering it. A diner, a gas station, and toilet buildings were crammed in a strip along the lot, but I parked facing the rows of semis.

Together, we sat in the car, peering out across the blacktop at the unlit cabs of trucks. Every so often, a figure would emerge from those dim places, long-legged and stumbling, stretched out even more by the twin glow of headlights until their silhouette hardly looked human.

Gabe shifted uneasily in his seat, drumming his fingers on his Styrofoam soda cup. We had gone to Burger King on our way out and bought hamburgers that I knew I wouldn't eat, my stomach already in turmoil.

He turned to me. "Why'd you want to come here? This about the mirror?"

"Yeah." I paused. "No."

"Then what?"

"I've been coming here for the last year, mostly on weekends but also during the week. My mom thinks . . ." I trailed off. "Actually, I don't know what she thinks. We don't talk like we used to."

Gabe looked at me, not comprehending. He hadn't understood why I kept a crowbar under the front passenger seat the first time he'd caught a glimpse of it, or what I wanted to use it for. How could he?

"She doesn't know, and my brother doesn't either. I wish they did, because part of me hates them for it. I mean, what kind of mother lets her teenage son take a seven-year-old to the amusement park alone? Seriously. What was she even thinking? That Brock would be a good babysitter? That he'd actually keep an eye on me?"

And the truth was that, deep down, I resented Brock for what he *hadn't* done. For not seeing it in my face when I found my way back to him in line, for not asking why I'd puked up my hot dog on the ride home. All he'd done was bitch at me for ruining his upholstery, and all this time, he'd never paid for his inattention. He'd never *suffered*. He just kept getting everything in life, rising higher in the world, and I couldn't stop feeling like I was gonna hit rock bottom any day now.

Gabe didn't answer, and I didn't look at him. We just sat there, our burgers growing cold, and let the silence fill the space between us until I found the words to continue.

"I don't remember it well anymore—it's more of a *feeling*, an idea of what happened, like watching it happen to someone else—but the guy in the restroom, he asked me if I liked trucks, said that he drove them for a living. That if I was good, he'd sit me down in his big shiny red truck and let me honk its horn. And it's all I have of him except, you know, the memory of what he did. And I mean, it wasn't even that bad what he did, you know? He didn't—" My voice caught in my throat like a clot of phlegm.

I couldn't say it. "He didn't do *that*. Was just a minute or two, and it was just a little rub and feel, but—but fuck, I was seven."

The air hissed between Gabe's teeth. "Shit, dude."

It wasn't funny, but I laughed before I could stop myself, because that was so like Gabe, so much what I needed in this moment. Still, I couldn't look him in the eye, so I tracked the lopsided flight of a white moth attracted to our headlights.

"You wanna know the real funny thing? Back when I was a kid, I used to daydream sometimes that he'd come take me away in his big red truck. That one day I'd open the door, and he'd be there, beaming down at me. And I'd just go with him, because—I don't know—because it's like Little Red Riding Hood. You know she knows it's a wolf, but she gets into her grandma's bed anyway."

Gabe reached down and placed his hand over mine, just for a moment. His fingers were so cold.

"I don't think that's how the story goes," he said.

"It's how the real one does."

Across the blacktop, I watched the shadowed figures do their walk, strut stilt-like toward blinking headlights or clamber down from truck cabs. Mostly girls and women, but every few visits, I'd spot a boy. Some were young enough that they could've gone to my school. It always made my stomach cold and leaden to think about how someone might end up here, and it scared me. It scared me to know that I was no different from them, not where it mattered anyway.

I got the same feeling when I drove past disheveled panhandlers at the roundabout or watched documentaries about missing teens or suicides—that this could be me one day, that we were made of the same blood. That there was something wrong with me, that he'd *given* me, and I was rotten, and it was only a long way down from here.

Chances were, the man hadn't even been a trucker at all. He could've lied about the truck. He could've been a fireman for all I knew. But I'd imagined more than once what I would do if I found him here, unchanged despite the years. I would stride up to him and I would put the crowbar to his head, again and again, until he was just blood and broken shards.

I didn't know why it hurt so much, why I was still so *angry*. It could have been worse, it could've been far worse, it'd been nothing I hadn't done to myself, so why was it so hard to just *let it go?*

About twenty feet down, a semi pulled into the spot facing us, its chrome grill flashing like a grin. The headlights blinked twice at us, then twice again, like the driver was coming on to us, saying come right up, get inside. The red hood was so shiny, I could see my white Hyundai reflected in its surface.

High up in the cab, the man was just a silhouette. He opened the truck door. By the time he climbed down, my eyes had adjusted enough that I could make out the tufts of bottle-blond hair sticking out from under his mesh trucker's cap. It was the kind of hat you could've bought at any gas stop between here and

Jax, but before I knew it, I was reaching for the crowbar under Gabe's seat, pushing his leg out of the way to get to it.

I tugged the tool free as Gabe stared slack-jawed at me. It felt like fate, see, and maybe it didn't even have to be the same man. Maybe it just needed to be someone who looked like him.

I staggered out of the car, grinding my dropped burger to mush beneath my heel. As I crossed the lot, thunder rumbled overhead. A thin arterial spray of lightning gushed across the sky, outlining the trucker's stark, straight-shouldered form as he walked toward the turnpike.

Behind me, Gabe called my name, but I didn't look back. With each step, the man's form solidified—a brown quilted jacket, faded Levi's stained at the seat with flecks of tan paint.

Him. My breath hissed through my clenched teeth. It was him.

As I came within five feet of the trucker, a sudden roar filled my ears. The man turned, and his eyes glowed with such brightness, his entire face was eclipsed by the searing white light.

He surged toward me with sickening velocity. Right before he reached me, a powerful force struck me from the side, throwing me off balance. Hands seized my shoulders. I hit the pavement, watching in stunned silence as a semitruck bored through where I'd been standing moments before. Not the red truck—the red truck wasn't even there anymore, if it'd even been there in the first place.

Sprawled on his knees beside me, still holding my arm, Gabe coughed violently. He wiped his mouth with the side of his hand, came back with blood misting his skin. I stared at him, my throat tight, like maybe cancer was catching.

"Marlow, what were you thinking?" His fingers were trembling so hard, he could hardly keep his grip. "I mean it. The hell?"

"I saw him," I whispered.

Two minutes later, as we were limping back to my car, my cell phone rang.

"It was my stepdad." Sarah sank onto the porch swing, her fingers tracing over the dents in her baseball bat's aluminum barrel. She hadn't looked at us once since opening her front door, just stepped out with the bat in hand. The urine-yellow glow of the bug light jaundiced her face and gouged deep shadows into her cheeks. "He was in the mirror again. Closer this time."

"Marlow saw something too," Gabe said, and Sarah lifted her eyes to me. Her irises were glazed with cataracts of sulphuric light.

"You did?" she asked, and I told it to her in pieces, the way she'd once confided in Gabe and me. It wasn't all—I didn't need to tell them all, they didn't deserve to know every detail or anything at all—but it was enough for sorrow to well in her eyes. I hated her pity, even though I felt the same for her and wished I could take her pain onto myself. Once I was done, she shook her head. "I'm so sorry, Marlow."

"Yeah." Her words made my tongue feel clumsy and too large for my mouth. I had to take a moment to swallow. "Thanks. I know."

Gabe rested against the porch railing, under the purple curtain of wisteria blossoms. "I think that somehow, whatever this thing is, whatever it wants, it can see what's happened to us. The worst thing, the thing that pierces to the core. It knows just how to hurt us the most."

"But why?" Sarah asked. "What did we do? We didn't deserve this."

"Maybe that's how it feeds," I said at last. Besides, she and Gabe knew as well as I did, it didn't mean a good goddamn whether we deserved it or not. There was no scale of justice in life.

Slowly, Sarah rose to her feet and gestured us inside. As we headed deeper into the house, past the cheerfully painted kitchen with its kitschy rooster salt and pepper shakers, past the overstuffed corduroy couch in the living room, I couldn't shake the feeling her mom wouldn't be coming home tonight. And all those houses down the street, they'd be empty too. No people, just lights blazing and TVs turned to static snow.

Shards of glass littered the hallway rug. On the wall, the mirror's frame gaped dumbly.

"I broke all the mirrors before you came." Sarah's fingers traced restlessly over the electrical tape wound around her baseball bat's handle. "The last one, the one in my bedroom, he was so close."

We went from room to room, peering under the beds and in the corners, hunting for shadows the way children would. As I brushed aside the dresses in her mom's closet, I half expected a pale face to emerge from between the layers of cotton and nylon—rheumy blue eyes and a fox's sly smile, one finger to his lips to shush the words that welled on my tongue, the other hand reaching downward.

At last, we came to her bedroom. Her mirror was cratered inward like a shrieking mouth, a needle-toothed maw of shards surrounding the black plastic beneath. I touched the jagged edges, not hard enough to cut myself, just to feel the promise of a bite. The surface was tacky to the touch, and when I pulled my hand away, my palm came back glistening red.

"Marlow." Sarah swore under her breath. "There's a first aid kit in the bathroom—"

"It's not mine." I rubbed the blood between my fingers. Still warm to the touch. "Your stepdad, you say he was close when you broke it?"

She shivered, her jaw cinching tight. "Close enough, I thought he was going to come through."

My gaze lowered to the bat clenched in her white-knuckled

fist. A dark stain dripped down the barrel. "I've got an idea."

The earthly remains of Black Rapids Amusement Park rotted just off the I-75, a moss-choked warren of rusty roller coasters and waterslides. It'd been closed five years now, and in that time, alligators and wild hogs had reclaimed the place.

It wasn't what happened to me in their restroom that did Black Rapids in, wasn't the recession, or the salmonella outbreak that put a horde of tourists in the hospital. Apparently, on one of the waterslides, there'd been an open section before a corkscrew turn, and a thirteen-year-old boy had hit the slide's top just right. His head came clean off, rolled down with all the rest. That was the killing blow.

The slide was gone now, but the demolition crew had done a half-assed job and left the stairs used to reach it, just going up to a platform that led nowhere. Rumor around town was that on Halloween night, if you managed to sneak inside the park and not become gator food in the process, that slide would be there again—coiled like an entrail along the water park's southern flank. And if you rode it down, it'd take you straight to Hell.

October was still months away, so I wasn't surprised when my flashlight beam skated across the platform but no slide. Rainwater filled the cement-lined pool the slide would've emptied into.

As we passed, I eyed the reflections our lights made in the stagnant water, waiting for the glowing beams to unspool into a nest of blond hair, a reaching hand, fingers like pale grubs. Instead the black surface glistened undisturbed, clotted with algae and lily pads.

My stomach knotted with tension, and each time I swallowed, it felt like there were loose teeth lodged in my throat. To keep my hands free, I clipped my old GI flashlight onto my jacket's breast pocket. It'd been a three-dollar thrift find, but its beam was stronger than any other light I'd got. I felt better with the crowbar in both hands.

"Are you sure it's even still here?" Sarah asked, flexing her fingers anxiously around her bat's handle.

"Yeah, it's here." I tore my gaze away from the water, turned back ahead. Gabe kept at my side like a shadow, weaponless except for a flashlight of his own. Our hollow footsteps were accompanied by the hum of mosquitos and the low *scritch-scratch* of animals creeping through the swampish overgrowth. The air was so heavy with the humidity of an approaching storm that the night actually seemed to have a physical weight to it, like the sky was boring down on us.

What I didn't tell Gabe or Sarah was that I'd been coming here ever since I got it in my mind to off myself. I didn't want to do the deed, but I wouldn't mind if an alligator snared me in a death roll or some slapdash structure came crashing down on my head. And yeah, maybe deep down I thought one of these days, I'd come across the guy, that he'd be waiting for me under the canopy of Spanish moss curtaining the merry-go-round or sitting with his stringy Levi's dangling in the brackish water, looking like no time had passed at all. He'd rise and come to me, offering me a fox's smile and sun-crinkled eyes. He'd hold out his hand, and I would take it.

Past the water park area, the amusement park welcomed us. A wooden roller coaster rising like a rib cage, the moss-tumored faces of the merry-go-round horses, hot dog stands and cart rides left to rot.

Gabe was panting so heavily, he had to stop and take a rest, just sit for a minute or two on one of the benches to regain his breath. He pushed his bangs out of his eyes and sloughed off an entire fistful of hair with it. He gazed down at the black clump, his mouth slack.

"I kept looking at my reflection in the water," he said as if that explained it all, his dazed eyes slowly lifting to me. There were a couple dark specks on his lips, dirt or maybe blood. His face was even thinner, as if he'd dropped another five pounds on the drive over.

I wanted to kiss him deep enough to reach his cancer and chew it out of him, starting with his lungs then moving on to his lymph nodes. I'd swallow the tumors down a bloody gobbet at a time, because I fucking deserved it, and I hated myself, and I was just so tired. I was so tired of feeling this way.

"Marlow," Sarah whispered, sinking her nails into my arm. I followed her gaze across the midway, to the live oaks lined down the sidewalk like a funeral procession, their gnarled branches draped in mossy veils.

A man in a shabby three-piece suit stepped slowly from the darkness, salt-and-pepper hair oiled back, his face—his face gleamed at us, perfectly blank and reflective, capturing our flashlights' beams and turning them back on us.

A mirror.

He had his belt folded in his hand. He struck it against his palm with a sharp *crack*. That sound told you all you needed to know, that when it hit you, it was gonna hurt like hell.

"Come on, let's go." I helped Gabe to his feet, testing his shoulder beneath my palm—so bony, as if there were just a scapula and joint under his cotton T-shirt sleeve, already sun-bleached and defleshed. And I shivered.

We hurried down the sidewalk, not at the run I would've liked, because Gabe wouldn't have been able to keep up with the way he was coughing and wheezing. When I glanced over my shoulder, the mirror-stepdad was walking slowly after us, still testing his belt in his palm.

Past the merry-go-round, the fun house loomed against the cloud-burdened sky. Its plyboard clown-head entrance yawned in a silent scream, candy-red lips gnawed on by termites and one lightbulb eye ruptured inward. When the ride was in motion, there'd be a moving tunnel past the clown mouth, slowly rotating so you'd have to shuffle along, back arched and head bowed. The tunnel stood at a standstill now, but it stretched on for longer than it should've, and with each step I took I felt as though I were shrinking down.

I felt so small.

Deeper in, used condoms were plastered to the floorboards like scraps of dead skin, and Gabe's flashlight beam revealed crumpled beer cans and uncapped syringes. I edged around him as we reached the end of the hall. Gripping the crowbar in both hands, I shouldered past the rubber streamers that formed the fun house's dangling entrails, and entered the mirror maze.

"Gabe, maybe you ought to wait for us out here," I said, but when I glanced back, he was holding a lead pipe he'd retrieved from the wreckage.

"What's the worst that can happen to me?" A thin laugh escaped his lips. "Cancer?"

I couldn't argue with that.

We continued deeper into the maze, in a single-file procession. Farther in, the air grew thick and stifling, and our footsteps were joined by the faint clang of a carnival jingle.

Maybe it would've been better to run, to allow Bloody Mary or whatever the hell this thing was to hunt us down one by one and hurt us the only way she knew how. We could become an urban legend, a cautionary tale. That was how all the movies went: It was the expected outcome. Everybody loved a good victim.

In the corner of my eye, a shadow oozed across a mirror. Swiveling around, I drove the hooked end of the crowbar into the pane, splitting my reflection down the middle and sending shards of glass cascading down. Behind it, there was another crooked corridor lined with even more mirrors. Turned toward me, they all presented the same reflection—my own features peering back, teeth bared and eyes flaring.

At the sight of my face, something broke inside me and my fear blazed into rage so incandescent, I thought it would tear me open from the chest down, spill out all that hatred in a steaming puddle.

"Screw you," I screamed, slamming the crowbar into the next frame. The glass only spiderwebbed this time, but I kept at it. "Screw you. *Screw you!*"

On the fourth blow, when the mirror did shatter, it revealed a hallway just as narrow and convoluted as the first, stretching off endlessly into the darkness. My face confronted me from a hundred different mirrors now, some staring back with the same wild-eyed terror, others frozen in agony or laughing hysterically, features twisted into a grotesque caricature of my own. The longer I looked at the reflections, the more I could feel my own face straining, my muscles struggling to mimic their distorted features.

I swung the crowbar again and again in a blind panic, my ears filled with the icy snap of breaking glass and, from a distance, shrieking laughter. Sometime after the tenth or fifteenth blow, I realized Sarah and Gabe weren't behind me, and I was alone with just my Rothco flashlight to peel back the darkness.

As the next mirror shattered beneath my crowbar, the fragments collapsed in a pile at my feet. Past the shard-toothed pane, *he* stood on the other side.

Quilted brown jacket, paint-speckled pants. Tufts of yellow hair peeked out from under his trucker's cap, the kind of unnatural shade you knew came from a bottle, and so thick and glossy, it almost looked plasticky. Like a wig, maybe. Or a scalp from one of his conquests.

His moist blue eyes met mine, and he smiled. What big teeth.

For years I had imagined what I could have done differently. What I should have done. The things I should've said, and the actions I could've taken. But what it always came back to was that there was nothing that would've made a difference, that it felt inevitable, as if he'd been waiting in that restroom all afternoon for me. It had felt predestined.

Tonight it felt the same way. He had been so big, but so was I now, and I could face him.

As the man took a step toward me, I swung the crowbar. His shoulder gave way, and the wet squelch of tearing flesh filled my ears. Crimson-stained cotton coated the crowbar's pronged end when I wrenched it free of him. A dark, glistening stream of blood gushed down his quilted jacket. It was as if the scent and sound had awoken something inside me, something that'd been incubating all this time, growing teeth, because I slammed the crowbar down again and again.

"You like this, don't you?" I screamed as his hand cracked with the brittle snap of broken glass. When the crowbar's hook caught on his mouth, his teeth scattered to the dust-caked floor, as jagged and metallic as mirror shards. "It feels good. *You like this.*"

I brought the crowbar down once more, aiming to cave his skull in, but he had vanished into the darkness. I was standing alone in a scatter of gore-stained glass, the crowbar's tip buried in the floor and my mouth as dry as bone. Blood oozed down my face in hot strands, and when I raked my hair back, my fingertips found even more repulsive souvenirs. Deeper into the mirror maze, Sarah called out to me: "Marlow, where are you?"

A shadow rippled over the mirrors, fleeing toward the sound of her voice. In its wake, it left a trail of bloody handprints across the metallic surface, ruby droplets welling from thin air as if the glass itself had sweated them.

"It's coming straight toward you, Sarah!" I shouted, racing after the mirror-presence. At the crossroad between two of the narrow mirror-lined passages, I nearly rammed into Gabe.

"That blood—" he began, but I shook my head, just kept

running. He followed after, and then we turned another sharp corner, and there Sarah was, bringing the baseball bat down on a man in a three-piece suit, with a mirror where a face ought to have been. Under her onslaught, the presence tried to jump to the next closest pane—dissolving into a smear of blood and shadow—but when it did, Gabe and I were there to greet it.

A spurt of blood gushed from the mirror as it shattered beneath Gabe's lead pipe. Using the crowbar, I pried the rest of the glass free, exposing a pulsing mat of flesh. No. Not just heaving flesh. I'd seen the same gristly clump in the photos Gabe had shown us, his lungs on glossy X-ray paper.

It was a tumor.

It took all three of us to wrench the throbbing, shapeless mass from the mirror's metal frame, digging in with our fingers when the pipe and baseball bat were useless, crushing the soft tissue to blood and pulp in our hands.

The creature didn't scream—it didn't make a sound at all—but I could tell we were hurting it. And I wanted to. I wanted to pour all my pain and hatred into its flesh until it *knew* what it was like to despise yourself. With each sopping chunk my crowbar tore free, the creature's writhing grew weaker and weaker, until at last its body went still.

Standing over what was left, I let the crowbar slip from my fingers, clatter to the floor. The three of us looked at each other, our faces hazed by the flash of sheet lightning that shone in through the rotten ceiling. Didn't know who was the first one to laugh, only that the laughter came over us all at once, until it bowed me over breathless and brought tears to my eyes.

As we hugged and knocked shoulders, I realized I'd never felt so alive. And deep down, I didn't want to die. I just didn't want to hurt anymore.

We made a pact that night. If Sarah's stepdad ever returned from Kentucky, we'd be there, waiting. If one day my monster rode up in his shiny red truck, there'd be three pairs of hands to wield the crowbar. And when the time came for Gabe, Sarah and I would break the mirrors one by one, draw the curtains tight, and turn off all the lights—until there were no more reflections, only the three of us and the encroaching dark.

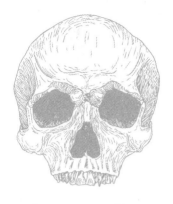

Truth or Dare

by Alex Brown

*T*RUTH: *I'M ONLY TELLING YOU THIS SO YOU DON'T MAKE THE* same mistake I did.

This isn't even about the tunnels. Not really. It's more about what happened *in* them. What I did. What he did. But I'm getting ahead of myself.

Before I go any further, it's important for you to know that no matter what some logical, boring person will try to tell you, the tunnels are real. The stories kids used to tell on the playground— hushed and hurried and secret—are true. The tunnels exist. Just like you and me.

The story goes like this:

A very long time ago, two people walked into the tunnels.

Only one walked out.

No one knows what really happened between them. Or what became of the one who was left behind. Depending on who you ask, the forgotten one wandered around the tunnels until they died. Probably starvation. Or lack of water. Or they walked into or off of something they had no business walking into or off of.

What we do know is this: The tunnels appear when there's a choice to be made. And that choice comes with a price. Something—or someone—has to be left behind.

I think you're smart enough to see where this is going. But before we get there, I should set the scene.

Sometime in the past, life went like this:

I met Dillon. Dillon met me.

I liked Dillon. Dillon liked me.

Or, at least, I thought he did.

I asked if he wanted to go on a date.

And he said: "Possibly."

I didn't think *possibly* was even an option. It seemed like a yes-or-no kind of thing for me.

And that was how we existed, Dillon and me. Drifting around each other like ships that had been tethered together in haste, because it was better than being alone. Both lost at sea, pulling the other in the opposite direction, going around and around in circles with no sign of land in sight.

Until the tunnels.

It was Dillon's fault. He asked the question. Forced me to make a choice.

He shouldn't have done that. He turned to me, taking my hand in his, raising it to his lips but lowering it before he kissed it (he would never kiss me, even though I wanted him to), and said, "I'm going away to college soon. Will you wait for me?"

And then the tunnels appeared.

I should have answered his question then and there. Instead I nodded toward the entrance and said, "I dare you to go into the tunnels with me."

He smiled and tossed his head back, laughing that laugh of his that I loved. Or thought I loved. And that, as someone once said, was all she wrote.

Well. It wasn't all I wrote. Or said. Or have left to say.

I know this is going to sound even more impossible, but we'd found the entrance to the tunnels once before. On the night I'd asked him out. The night he said *possibly*, and then—after he insisted that pineapple was a topping that deserved to be on a pizza—followed it up with *we're better as friends*, even though he was the one who started flirting with me. He was the one who made me feel wanted, when the only thing I'd ever known before was wanting *someone*.

Not anyone specific. Just . . . someone. Who agreed that pineapple didn't belong on pizza, or who wasn't afraid to walk up next to me in a crowded room, put their arm around my shoulders, and let everyone know that I was the one they chose.

I was the one who mattered.

The particulars of the someone weren't important—I'd always wanted the person, rather than what they looked like. Who they were. What they had. Or didn't have.

If I wanted to sound deeper than I was, it was more about someone's soul. If souls existed.

Maybe mine did. Once.

Maybe Dillon's did too.

We walked away from the tunnels that night and the entrance disappeared. But we kept what we saw a secret. Something that was just between us, that was another thing that could have happened, but it didn't, because that's how it always was between Dillon and me. He made me feel *wanted*, and he made me feel like I wanted *him*, but he never could quite want *me* in the way I needed him to.

I always wondered if the tunnels appeared that night because *he* was supposed to make a choice. Maybe he had to figure out what he wanted us to be, but he wasn't ready, and that's why, ever since, we'd always been everything and nothing to each other. Someone we didn't want to leave behind, because being alone was worse than being whatever we were when we were together.

But now things were different. The choice wasn't his to make. It was mine.

That night, we didn't linger in front of the entrance, talking about nothing in particular as the moon slid across the night sky. We didn't whisper stories in each other's ears, or brush our fingers together in the dark, or make promises to each other that we knew we'd never keep.

Instead he took my dare and walked right in without saying anything. And I followed.

The steady *drip drip drip* of water filled in the silence between us.

I wanted to say so many things. Ask him all the questions I'd been too scared to, because I knew the answer would mean the end of whatever we were.

I wanted to see if he loved me as much as I loved him.

But I couldn't. Not then, anyway. So instead I cleared my throat and said, "Truth or Dare?"

Without skipping a beat, he said, "Dare," because he always picked dare.

Dillon wasn't a truth kind of guy.

"I dare you to scream," I said. I didn't look at him. Instead I ran my hands over the walls, marveling at how the rocks around us had been smoothed out and paved over. Brushed and bruised and polished until they looked nothing like what they used to be.

"Really, Sienna?" he replied. There was subtext, though. There was always subtext with him.

In this case, it was: *Really, Sienna? If anyone else is around, then they'll know we're down here. Together.*

If I were brave, I would've told him that was the point. To announce to everyone that we were in the same place. Together.

But I wasn't brave. So I just said, "You heard me."

And then he screamed, because of course he did. He never turned down a dare.

The steady *drip drip drip* of water paused as Dillon's scream filled the space between us.

Before we continue, I have to apologize for something.

I didn't introduce myself to you. That was what always happened when Dillon was involved. He became the most important thing in my universe, and I faded away. I was a nameless player in my own story.

Until he decided to give me a name. That day—that *night* in the tunnels—it was Sienna. The day before, it was Ashleigh (yes, spelled like that), and the day before that it was Dawn.

Dillon knew my real name. But he never used it. He said it was our special thing.

He said it meant I could be a new person each day. Whoever I wanted to be.

But what he really meant was that I could be whoever *he* wanted me to be.

And I went along with it, because I loved him. One more game to add to the list.

Dillon loved games.

I thought I did too.

The steady *drip drip drip* of water stepped back in as Dillon's scream faded away. He turned to me, gesturing to the darkness ahead of us.

"Happy?" he asked.

I nodded, because I was.

I expected him to turn back around. To keep walking. But he didn't. He watched me, his icy blue eyes illuminated by his flashlight.

I couldn't hold his gaze for long. Not with my heart storming around in my chest and my palms getting so sweaty that I had to grip the flashlight tighter. I knew the choice was mine. But I didn't want to make it.

Instead I turned my gaze to the walls. I wasn't sure how many people had been in the tunnels before—who had to make the same choice I did—but I could get a rough idea from the initials carved into the cold, smooth façade.

What had all these people decided to leave behind? Were they happy now? Or had the tunnels made everything worse?

I ran my hands along the side of the wall, taking in the grooves and sharp edges of the initials. I couldn't ask any of them these questions. But I wanted to.

"We should keep going," I said, because I couldn't stand the silence any longer.

I moved first. His footsteps hesitated for a few seconds before he finally joined me.

There were no lights strung up on the ceiling, leaving a trail for us to follow. Aside from the small beams coming from our flashlights, we were surrounded by darkness.

The only sound in there—aside from our footsteps, our breathing, and Dillon's scream—was the steady *drip drip drip* of water.

I had no idea where it was coming from.

If you're familiar with the legends (and even if you're not), then you'd know (or wouldn't) that the tunnels ran underneath the town. But they always stopped short of the sea. As if they were afraid to touch it.

Were the stories wrong? Were we underneath the ocean? Or was the water coming from somewhere else?

I still don't know. Maybe I never will.

"What are we doing down here?" Dillon asked, still watching me.

"Playing Truth or Dare," I replied, because it was as honest as I wanted to be. "It's your turn."

A mix of mischief and resignation danced in his eyes. That was how he always looked at me. Like he was planning something but knew he'd never act on it.

There were so many times where I wanted him to act on it.

"Okay, Sienna," he said, his lips curling into a dangerous smile. "Truth or Dare."

And I said, "Truth," because it was all I ever wanted from him, but I knew it was something he'd never give me.

But he didn't like that answer. He never liked it when I tried to take a truth when all he ever wanted to do were dares.

So he said, "Oh, come on, do a dare instead. It's more fun."

And I said, "Okay, dare," because he wanted me to. I couldn't help it. That was just the way things were between us. He made up his mind and asked my opinion, but it was only ever as a courtesy. To make me feel like I was contributing to the conversation. That I had some value. That he cared. Not too much—or too little. He cared just the right amount to keep me around.

He cared just the right amount to give me hope.

"I dare you to turn your flashlight off and walk ahead without me," he said as the steady *drip drip drip* of water turned into something that sounded like a hiss.

"How far?" I asked.

"I'll let you know when to stop," he replied.

I didn't want to do it. But a dare was a dare, and all was fair in love and war and whatever we were, so I turned off my flashlight and walked past him.

I wanted him to reach out. To grab my arm and stop me. Or grab my arm and pull me into him. Wrap me in a hug or an embrace or whisper in my ear that he was only joking when he said we were better as friends. That he wanted us to be more now.

But he stood there, silently watching. Never there for me

when I needed him.

Only there when he wanted to be.

The steady *drip drip drip* of water accompanied me as I stepped into complete darkness.

Pressing forward, always forward. Never back. Dillon hadn't told me to turn around, so I couldn't. If I did, it would prove that I didn't love him. Failing at one simple task—not being able to do what was asked of me—that wasn't love. I had to be everything to him at all times, even when he refused to do the same for me.

That was how it had always been.

But I didn't want that anymore.

I told you before that you could probably see where this was going. Well, here it is: I went into the tunnels to leave my feelings for Dillon behind.

He'd asked me to wait for him, but I couldn't.

I loved him—or, at least, I thought I did—but sometime between him telling me we were better as friends and me daring him to come into the tunnels with me, I'd figured out that it wasn't the kind of love I wanted.

Love wasn't supposed to make you so nauseous that you couldn't eat. It wasn't supposed to leave you feeling empty. Constantly worried that you said or did the wrong thing.

That you weren't enough, and never would be.

Love wouldn't send you into a dark tunnel without a flashlight.

And that was why, when I knew I was far enough away for

him not to see it, I turned my flashlight back on.

I'd always wondered what happened to the people in the original story. If the one who did the leaving was happy with their choice. If their life was better. If they had no regrets.

And what happened to the one who was left behind? Were they doomed to wander the tunnels until they died? Or did the darkness swallow them whole and spit them out as something new?

No one will ever know the real answer. I suppose it's up to whoever tells the story.

The steady *drip drip drip* of water kept me company as I looked around. Something tugged at the spot behind my heart, right beneath my ribs. It pulled me forward, then a few steps to the right, around another corner, then to the left to make another turn. And that's when I found it.

A skull.

I picked it up because it felt like the right thing to do. I brought the hole where its ear would be up to my mouth and whispered, "I can't love him anymore." And then added a "please," to be polite. It never hurt to be polite.

I carried the skull with me for a little while, still going farther into the tunnels. Maybe he'd tried to call me back. Sensed that, for once, I was okay without him. Maybe he could feel his hold on me slipping out of his hands. Or he was tired of being alone and I was the easiest way to pass the time. To fill in the emptiness around him.

There was always so much emptiness around him.

Maybe, after he called me for a few minutes and I didn't reappear, he walked into the darkness too. I wasn't going to call out or give him a sign or help him in any way. I'd chased him for long enough. It was his turn to chase me.

I was still holding on to the skull when I found the door. If you're confused by this detail, then I apologize. I must not have told you about it earlier.

The door appears when the choice is ready to be made. When the chooser has finally made up their mind about what they're going to do.

What they're willing to leave behind.

I thought it would look old. Or have more initials carved into it, like the walls around me. But it was bright red. Almost new. Waiting for me to open it.

The skull sat heavy in my hands as I stood there, weighing my options. I could turn around and try to find Dillon. I could keep going deeper into the tunnels, past the door. Refuse to make the choice at all.

Or I could walk through it. Do the thing I went there to do.

The steady *drip drip drip* of water marked time as I fluttered between each choice.

Going back to Dillon didn't make sense. Not when my feelings still hadn't changed. I had to leave them behind—but I wasn't sure I was ready.

Heading deeper into the tunnels was the only option. Putting more distance between Dillon and me was a good idea. Allegedly. Maybe.

Possibly.

Even though I was there to forget about how hot my skin burned every time we almost touched—or how I never could figure out if I wanted to run toward him or away from him—part of me still wished he were there beside me. I knew that part was wrong. That it was mistaken. That maybe Dillon was good for somebody else. Anybody else. But not me.

Never me.

It wasn't fair. Or right. It didn't make sense to hold out hope that he'd change. Or he'd care. Or he'd take back everything he ever said. All those times he made me wonder if I would ever be good enough for someone to love.

The steady *drip drip drip* of water wrapped around me as a voice hissed, from somewhere in the darkness, *"You have a choice to make."*

But I didn't reply, because I wasn't ready to think about that.

Yes, it was the whole reason I went into the tunnels in the first place. I know that. You know it. Maybe Dillon even knew it, and that was why he agreed so easily. Maybe he was ready for me to move on. He was only trying to be supportive.

Not in a way I wanted or needed. But he did what was best for him and I went along with it, because that was just how things were between Dillon and me.

The steady *drip drip drip* of water accompanied another statement from something in the darkness. *"It's almost time,"* it said. And I didn't know what to reply, so I kept walking.

I wasn't trying to be rude or ungrateful or anything like that.

It's just . . . it's one thing to promise yourself you're going to do something, and another to actually see it through.

I knew that things would be better if I stopped loving him. I knew that *love* wasn't even the word to describe what we had, no matter how much I wanted it to be. I'd spent so long talking myself into believing it. But there was a small part of me that screamed every time I thought the word.

And that was why I knew I had to do it. He would be erased from my life because I didn't want any part of me to scream ever again.

"Sienna?" Dillon's voice called out, from somewhere behind me. "Where are you? You can come back now. The dare's done."

He was wrong. The dare wasn't done.

The steady *drip drip drip* of water covered my footsteps as I moved forward. Away from him and closer to the decision I'd made.

The water was my accomplice. Even though I didn't know where it was coming from. Not that it mattered.

"Sienna, this isn't funny," he insisted, and I agreed. It wasn't funny. But it was happening.

"Come back," he said softly. Too softly for me to hear, but

I heard it anyway. "Please," he added, as if that word would change everything.

As if *please* would be enough to erase everything he'd put me through. Everything I'd put myself through, in order to keep him.

But that was the problem, wasn't it?

It was impossible to keep something that never intended to stay.

No. It was more than impossible. It was exhausting. Heartbreaking. The kind of thing that tore you to shreds, only to hastily put you back together, with no regard to where the pieces were being placed. It was a painful process. A punishment.

The steady *drip drip drip* of water confirmed what I already knew: I was tired of being punished.

"If you don't turn back now—if you don't find me—I'll leave," he said, offering up an ultimatum like it meant something. It didn't. Not anymore.

The steady *drip drip drip* of water filled in the silence between us as something else called out to me from the darkness. *"Have you decided?"* it asked.

"Yes," I replied, because deep down inside, I'd had it all figured out from the moment I met Dillon and Dillon met me.

"Sienna?" Dillon shouted. "Is that you?"

"Of course," I replied. "Who else would it be?"

I thought that was a fair question. There was no one else in the tunnels but us, after all.

If it seems like I was ignoring the disembodied voice, it's because I was. Like most things I don't know or can't place, I find it best to pretend they never existed at all.

"Where are you?" he asked.

"Follow my voice," I replied.

And that was how we carried on for a little while. Another game to add to our list.

When he finally found me—when I allowed him to catch up with me—I was standing in front of the red door. I gently placed the skull next to my feet as he walked into my flashlight's narrow beam.

"What's that?" he asked.

"A door," I replied.

"No shit."

I shrugged. "Ask a simple question, get a simple answer."

The steady *drip drip drip* of water crashed around us as the narrow beam cast by his flashlight blinked in and out of existence. He didn't speak again until it came back to life.

And when it did, he said, "What's it doing here?"

I shrugged again. "Probably waiting for someone to open it."

He thought about what I said for a few seconds—which may have been the longest amount of time he'd ever dedicated to anything I'd said—and smirked. What came out of his mouth wasn't surprising at all.

Disappointing, maybe. But not surprising.

"I dare you to open the door," he said.

I shook my head. "No."

"No?"

"That's not how the game works, Dillon," I said, and from the way he looked anywhere but at me, he knew I was right. "You dared me to walk around these tunnels alone. It's your turn to do something."

The steady *drip drip drip* of water filled me with the confidence I needed to say, "Truth or Dare?"

And, for the first time since I met Dillon and Dillon met me, he replied with, "Truth."

This wasn't because he was feeling particularly truthful. Or that he had something he needed to get off his chest. We both understood what he meant as soon as the word fell out of his mouth: Only one of us was going to open that door. And it wouldn't be him.

Like I said before, I wasn't surprised by his answer. Just sad that this was the only way for me to ask him a question. One I'd needed an answer to for way too long.

The steady *drip drip drip* of water stood firmly beside me as I said, "Did you ever love me?"

"No," he said, too quickly, because maybe he knew me better than I thought. "Yes. Maybe? It's . . . complicated."

"I don't think it is. I loved you." The steady *drip drip drip* of water pushed me to add. "Or, at least, I thought I did."

He threw an uneasy smile my way. "Love isn't something I'm trying to do. Not right now, anyway."

"But it will be? Eventually?"

He shrugged. "Possibly."

There it was again. That word. A way for him to leave a door open that he never intended to step through. A promise he never meant to keep.

"Possibly," I repeated. "But not with me."

"It could be—"

"No," I said, interrupting him. "You don't have to pretend. It's okay. Really."

"Really?" he asked, disappointment coloring his tone. There was a hint of annoyance, too. Like *I'd* been the one who'd done something wrong. Like *I'd* made a mistake by drawing a line. Making a boundary. Telling him that I was done—that we were through—without actually saying the words.

It was always my fault. At least, it was when we were together.

The steady *drip drip drip* of water raged next to me as I calmly replied, "Really. Thank you for being honest."

I didn't add *for once* in there, but it was implied.

He nodded. "I'm glad we got that cleared up." He took a few steps toward me, holding out a hand. "We're good? Nothing's changed?"

"We're good. Nothing's changed," I replied, taking his hand. There was a time when his touch would have set my skin on fire.

Now it just made it crawl. "In fact, I think it's my turn to play the game."

There it was. The smirk that I thought I loved so much. "Okay, Sienna," he said, pulling his hand away from mine. "Truth or Dare?"

"Dare," I said, because even though I was always a truth kind of girl, Dillon wasn't a truth kind of guy.

"I dare you to open that door," he said, because he was nothing if not predictable.

"Are you sure you want me to?" I asked. "What if you don't like what's on the other side?"

"Only one way to find out, right?"

The steady *drip drip drip* of water crescendoed around us as I said, "Right."

I got one last good look at him, remembering every feeling I'd ever had. How desperate I was to make him laugh, because that was the only sound that made my heart soar. How it felt like home whenever he said my name. Not one of the fake ones.

My real name.

How all he had to do was smile and I'd forgive everything else. The hurt. The confusion. The times where I felt sick, or sad, or worse: like I was making all of it up.

How he barely knew what I needed or wanted because all we'd ever talked about was what he needed and wanted.

How he'd never love me, no matter how much I wanted him to.

How I'd never loved him, no matter how much I wanted to.

The steady *drip drip drip* of water walked with me as I strode right up to the bright red door.

The steady *drip drip drip* of water wrapped around my hand as my fingers curled around the knob.

The steady *drip drip drip* of water vanished as I threw the door open and made my choice.

Silence—only silence—filled the space between Dillon and me.

Until he broke it.

Just like he broke me.

"That's . . . not what I expected," he said, walking closer to the door—closer to me—but not *too* close.

He was right. It wasn't what I'd expected either.

There was nothing on the other side of the door. Just more tunnels.

But sometimes life gives you things you don't expect, and you have to make the best of them. Sometimes life puts pineapple on pizza, even when you hate pineapple on pizza, and you have to painstakingly pick each of those little slivers of fruit off until your pizza is finally pineapple free.

But it's never completely free. The pineapple juices seep into the cheese, ruining it.

The pizza is never the same.

"What should we do?" he asked as the steady *drip drip drip* of water sounded from the other side of the door.

I'd already made my choice. I wasn't going to change my mind.

That didn't make this next part any easier, though.

There's an alternative to painstakingly picking every last bit of pineapple off of your now-ruined pizza. You can throw the whole thing away.

Or, if you don't want to be as wasteful, you can give it to someone else.

A shadow lingered behind Dillon. Growing larger and larger until it swallowed up the rest of the tunnels behind him.

"This was never going to be our door. Only mine," I replied, stepping through it and right into a puddle. Water pooled at my feet. It seeped into my shoes and socks as I said, "Find your own."

My fingers curled around the knob. I slammed it shut.

"Sienna," he said, pounding on the door as something between a growl and a scream sounded from behind him. "Let me in. Please!"

I didn't have to see through to the other side to know what was happening. Whatever was in the tunnels was claiming him.

It seemed fitting, since he could never claim me.

"Goodbye, Dillon," I said as the growl turned into something that sounded like the steady *whoosh* and *rush* and *roar* of water. Whatever was in there with him was flooding his side of the door. "And good luck."

He didn't have anything to say after that.

Before you ask, I don't know where the water came from. Or what happened to Dillon. There are some mysteries that have to stay that way. Some questions that are best left unanswered. Some people who you have to leave behind, because they were never any good for you in the first place.

And that's okay. The leaving-people-behind bit, I mean.

There's a version of this story where he found his own way out, and one where he didn't. But I'll leave that one up to you. It was never my decision to make anyway.

And—even though I'm only telling you this so you don't make the same mistake as I did—it's okay if you already have. Or if you will. Sometimes we try our best to avoid bad people and heartbreaking situations, but the bad people and the heartbreak come anyway.

What's important to remember is this: If you have a choice to make, the tunnels will appear to you. But you shouldn't go inside unless you have something you'd like to leave behind.

That's also the last thing I need to apologize to you for.

You see, I told you that I was always a truth kind of girl, and Dillon never a truth kind of guy.

There was a small lie in there. A lie of omission, technically, but still. A lie's a lie.

When I went into the tunnels that night, I *did* want to lose my feelings for Dillon. But that wasn't everything.

I wanted to lose him, too.

And I did.

My choice was never if I would wait for him while he went off to college. It was whether or not I would keep caring about him in a way that slowly destroyed everything I was or could be.

My choice was simple: him or me.

I hope you can understand why I did it. It's fine if you don't, though. If I had to do it all over again, I would.

But I've been talking for too long, and we were in the middle of a game, weren't we?

I think it's your turn.

Truth or Dare?

The Burning One

by Shakira Toussaint

WE LIVE UP HIGH, EH?

Past tree stump and tree trunk and treetop and leaf. Up rock wall and rock steps, up boulder on pebble. We live high, high on the mountain on a ledge on a cliff, next to cloud and as close to sun as you can be before it burn you right up.

Our mountain is the only one. Right in the middle of the land, so all can see and be seen. But there's no one else. Just me and Mama, and the bugs and animals and the thing Below that screams.

Mama says we born on the mountain and it's mountain we die on. She says we stay High and we safe. And I does listen, eh? I hear the thing Below that yells and I know I safe on the mountain up High, but sometimes I think of Below, when the screeching thing is quiet and sleeping. I think what it might be like to touch the leaves and feel the brown mud in between my toes instead of mountain rock. And I wish.

We have a little stream up High. A little trickle of water that comes from the mountaintop. But I see there's a sparkle of water Below, hidden between some trees that grow close. Often I think if it's small like our little stream or big and wide and deep enough to fall into. I wonder what it feel like, to walk into it until it hits my chin, to dip my head below its surface.

She catch me staring one day, Mama does.

"What you watch?" she asks.

I'm leaning over the cliff, arms dangling, feeling the air.

"I does look at the shine," I say, pointing to it. "I like to see it wink between the trees."

She's quiet for a while, too quiet. So I roll onto my back and squint up at her. Sun in front of us now. So the long shadow she usually has is pulled tight to her feet. I move mine, squirming close to set my toes into the sliver of dark to keep them cool.

Her long face pulls longer, and I know what she say before she say it.

"Make sure all you do is watch," she snaps. "Because up High we safe, y'hear? Nothing good Below. Nothing good."

I nod and she copy the movement and turns, taking her shade for my toes and her warning with her. But still I curl back onto my stomach and watch the twinkle between the tree trunks and leaves. I think maybe I—but the thing Below wake, eh? It wake with a screeching yowl and I forget about my twinkle, and what it might feel like soothing my sun-hot skin.

She built our home, she told me. All before there was rock, until Mama carried me up and smashed the rock to carve our cave. She spends most of her time there, killing the meat we eat, cutting its skin from flesh to use for clothes, hollowing the coconuts we drink for bowls. She tall, my mama. Tall and thin and strong.

I does like to watch Below from the cliff. I like the way the leafs they do move on some breeze that don't reach my face. If I look close enough, the trees themselves move too. Twisting, curling, growing, dying. I watch them smallest, small, big, bigger, then brown to black to taken by some angry mash of wind that tears it from base and root up from the ground and fling it aside to rot.

All around I see green. No matter if I in our cave or on the other side of the mountain, digging my fingers deep into the rock to keep myself attached as I peer around. Still, all is green and beyond, a line of yellow sand and then a blue line that ring the land and beyond on all sides.

The *sea*.

If I try, I can see the water ripple and curl, sometimes calm, sometimes mad and frothing white as it lashes the land. But always it stays. Never mad enough to breach the yellow sand and come to land. It like me and Mama and Below, the land and sea. Always separate.

Until one night a storm roll in.

The kind that pick the trees from their roots. Our cave keeps us dry—and we two stay huddled in a corner to keep warm. When the wind dies, we crawl out on hand and knee because the rock is slippery and wet, and I see what waits for us.

Sea has finally broken its binds and pushed something onto land.

The thing look strange, like wood all curled together with cloth attached to poles—it's tangled in the trees and the sand. I would have been satisfied with that. I would have watched this new thing until I was old like Mama. But there was something else on the shore. People. Ones like me and Mama and others, bigger with flat chests and short hair. All clustered and shivering or shouting or sitting as others ran around the wrecked thing and pulled things out of it.

When I see these new things, a funny thing happens in my stomach. An empty-tighty feel begins. Small, at the back. Like I don't eat for weeks. It makes me stand and step toward the new people.

I'm so mesmerized—so interested that I don't know I'm about

to step off the cliff ledge until Mama's strong, bony hand is curled around my arm and she yanks me back hard, dragging me till my feet cuts on the wet rock.

She throws me into our cave and stands at the mouth, backed by remnants of lightning and bright moon shining through the gray clouds. The empty feel inside is gone. Outside, the thing Below yells into the wind.

Her chest heaves as she spits: "Stay up High!"

So much time passes as I watch the new people—sometimes I don't sleep for days and days. I watch as they gather things from what Mama calls a *ship* and they drag things she calls *carriages*, by new beasts called *horses*. And they small ones grow big and the first *men* and *women* change from plump to frail.

I watch as they build along the coast, and then one day, I watch as a smaller group leaves and come inland, leaving the coast behind to move into the green wood that surrounds Home.

All day does Mama watch me watch them. If I get too close to the edge, she calls me back, if I watch too long she pulls me back to sleep in our cave and each time I go willingly she smiles and I smile too but I don't tell her what I does think. Which is that I wish I was down Below, watching them close. Walking with them close.

It takes them weeks, but the small group finally comes close to the base of our mountain. I scuttle round the back to watch them as they pass over the day, hanging off the rock by my fingers.

They walk deep into the woods, and make camp by my sparkle of water. My heart thumps once, hard. They so *close*. Close enough that when a wind snaps up the cliff, I think I can almost smell their sour skin.

It takes them a long time to build their houses. One by one the trees where they first make camp fall, and I know no more will rise to take their places.

It's only when they're settled and all the trees are gone that Mama picks her day to leave.

Our meat is running low, and she needs to hunt. I'm not allowed to go with her, but if I good, she say she bring me two rabbits to eat. They're my favorite—but they live far on the other side of the land. It will take her three days there and back. Usually I'm upset when she leaves, but this time I think of the people by my sparkle, and saliva pools in the mouth at the thought.

"And you stay here, yeah?" she says, one foot on a rock step, one foot in Home. "You stay up High where it safe?"

I nod, careful not to look Below to where the people are. I can hear them, though. Can hear the tin of their voices and the crackle of their fires. Saliva fills my mouth and a new ache starts in my jaw that makes me wince.

Mama sees though, and her foot comes off the rock step. "What's that?" she asks, hand curling around the strap of her leather pouch. "What's wrong with you?"

She's going to stay, I think, worried. She thinks I'm sick, so she'll stay and then—and then . . .

I swallow, shake my head. I thinking nonsense now. And then what? I climb down the steps that Mama's feet make and sneak past the Beast Below and . . . talk to them? What I say?

"I fine," I say, and smile. Her hand uncurls and her foot slides back onto the step and my chest feels less tight.

She nods, turns to walk down the first few steps, then twists her neck to give me one of her lovely smiles. "I be back soon, eh? You stay High. You stay safe."

"Yes, Mama," I echo. "I stay High. I stay safe."

It take me all of one day before I make my way down. I pace and turn and try to sleep the feeling away, but the longer I say no, the more my gums hurt and the pinching in my stomach grows so terrible, I cry out for Mama but she's too far to hear.

She don't hear or see as good as me and for the first time in a long time, I terror. I try to eat the last of our dried meat, but it taste like ash in my mouth and I spit it out. I try to drink water from our little stream, but it doesn't help either.

So I stand at the top of our rock steps and swallow three times before running down them. It takes Mama hours to get down them, but I do it quick, yeah? Quick I run until the last step and then I hear Mama, just like if she right beside me.

Up High safe. Nothing good come from Below.

But I come this far, and my stomach hurts so bad that I ignore her till she quiet.

The thing Below screams once, twice, three times then it quiets so loud, I think the ground might open to eat me whole, but then it quiets too so I take my wobble-step Below. As soon as I do, my stomach settles and my gums cool. I squidge my feet into the damp earth, stamping in the mud until it flicks up my legs and I laugh, feeling good for the first time since Mama left.

I rub my hands into the dirt then trace up the trunk of the tree that I've watched grow over the years, and jump high to flick the wet leaves with my hand. They feel strange, like thin rock, and if I push my ear against the trunk, I can almost hear the same, slow beat from inside my own chest.

A cry distracts me and for a moment I think it the Beast. I think of High and Home and our cave and what I've left behind and how angry Mama will be when she gets back.

I should go. I feel better now. I should go, I think, but the cry comes again, and I realize it's not the Beast and soon I'm running, pushing past trees whose trunks crack, to get to the cry, and emerge by a small, muddy pool I've never seen from High.

It's not as pretty as my sparkle, but I'm less interested in it than I am with what's inside it.

No breasts, square jaw and tan, like the underside of a boar before you slice its neck. A boy, Mama had called them.

He looks to me, opens his mouth to two rows of blunt teeth. I swash my tongue over my own that taper slightly to points. How he eat meat with teeth so square? I think, confused.

He tries to talk. It takes him six times before he realizes that I do not understand. But his words *strange*. All mash and harsh. Not like the music that Mama makes or the music she taught me. He speaks like each word is crack of thunder.

My eyes sharp, though. I see what he cannot through the murk of the water—his leg is caught in a vine. Each time he twists or calls for help, it drags him deeper. I watch until he grows desperate before I wade into the muddy water. I don't go far. I don't know if I can float or if I'll sink to the bottom and Mama will wonder forever why I left her. I only go as far as my chin, then I hold my breath, reach down beneath the muck, and snap the tree root that has him trapped.

He scrambles back onto the bank, wet and dirty, gasping for air. If I listen hard enough, I can hear the flutter of his little heart in his chest. Fast and faint. Not slow and strong like mine or the trees.

I move too, walk out of the water and back onto land, happy as happy to feel my toes squelch and sink into the wet earth.

He says something, a crash of words forcing its way out of his mouth, but I can't understand and eventually he stops trying, just stares and stares until my skin pricks and my gums burn.

It's so sudden that I turn, flee back into the woods, up the rock steps to Home. I wash my feet in our stream, and the water turns brown to black to clear again as all Below is washed away. When I sleep that night, I think of the boy.

Before sleep takes me, the Beast gives one long wail into the night.

Mama comes back on the fourth day.

Her eyes sharp, yeah? They swoop and circle around and on me and Home, but Below is gone and she grunts, satisfied, and throws a rabbit at my feet and stomps off.

I don't see the boy (*my* boy) again for a long time. Mama goes and comes three times before I feel the tightness in my stomach, the hurt in my gums, and know I have to go again.

Mama dresses to hunt and then makes to leave, turning at the steps again to squint at me in the sun.

"Stay High," she calls.

"Stay safe," I answer.

I wait for a moon to pass before I descend, skirting around the thing Below that screeches, ignoring its cattle-wails, and walk until I see the village come close.

It's bigger now. More houses, more people. In the moonlight

I see my water twinkle between the trees in the distance and I turn, try to walk to see if I can finally view it, but I hear the snap of a twig, the crunch of a foot, and whirl and see the boy. *My* boy.

He's older. There's a dust of hair on his chin. When I squint, I can see each short strand.

I crouch, and he stops. A slip of moonlight makes him look even paler than he was before. Not dark like me or Mama.

He speaks. His voice is deeper now. More harsh. As he speaks, he walks slowly to me, and I inch back until my spine finds a tree and he stops, just shy of me. His smell wafts over, it's tart, like ripe coconut or meat the hour before it turn bad.

He huffs and his mouth twists like Mama's does when she find me watching Below too long and I know he angry. He tries to speak again, but another voice joins him—deeper, older. Coming fast from his back. I listen hard, hear the feet, hear the weak, fast heart, and I go, even as he calls after me.

My teeth ache all the time. I can't wait long to see him again. I won't. So I throw my meat off the cliff edge of Home and spoil what supplies I can when Mama isn't watching.

I know it wrong, but I want to see him and Mama has to be gone for that to happen. She watch me strangely, though. Ask me strange things.

"You hungry for more?" "You want something else?" "Meat too dry?"

I say No, Mama, No, Mama, Yes, Mama.

It the last one that makes her eyes narrow, make her watch me too close so next time she ask I say No, Mama, and she smile and leave.

When he see me, he smiles. Big, untroubled. Like Mama if she didn't worry all the time. He calls to me and my gums throb once then not again.

I follow him, away from my mountain and the smell of Mama and the Beast that screams every step away I take.

He weaves us through the forest, and not being High, I confuse as to where we are until I see the sparkle through the bush and then I'm running, pushing past him to break through the trees, and finally I see my sparkle.

It's bigger than I thought, wide and deep and blue, even in the moonlight. He taps my shoulder and I shudder, wince. He sees and smiles sad this time and points to a cloth on the floor. There's food laid out, and he takes my hand. His is rough and large and mine is stiff in his grip.

The pinch in my stomach flares once and then dies. He makes me sit and I do, stiff, not fluid like him. My bones used to rock, not earth.

He offers me food, but I shake my head and watch as he eats bite after bite. I like the way the food looks at his neck, bulging at his throat before it goes down. There's a vein in his neck that beats in time with his little heart and I watch it until he waves his hands to get my attention.

He taps his chest. "E-li-as." He says it again and again until I repeat it back. Then he points to me. But if I have name, it gone now, so I say nothing.

So he looks at me and points and says, "Lov-lay."

So I take his Lov-lay and lick my lips when the vein at his neck jumps.

I want to see him all the time. And I do. I ruin coconut shell bowls and I throw all the food off the mountain. I do anything to make Mama leave so that I can go and see him. And each time I see him, the more I want to see him again.

He starts to bring me a single flower and I keep each one, even after they brown and crack and they die. I bring him things too. A boar I hunted and killed. An agouti I find on the branch of a tree that I stun. I bring him pretty pebbles and funny leafs I find. He teaches me his words, and I feel sick when I say them back, but it makes him smile to hear them in my mouth, so I do it even when my jaw hurts around the sound of them.

I sometimes make him watch with me. At streams, at leafs. One day I make him watch the ants with me and just as I turn to say See? Look how they work together, I find him watching me. Always me. Never the ants or what I want to show him.

E-li-as and Lov-lay. That's what I say in my head between Mama being back and me being High. I spend so long Below that the thing that screeches quiets and the thirst in my stomach grows so terribly that I want to see E-li-as all the time to make it go away.

One day, he keeises me. That's what he call it.

Keeis.

The word long and strange, just like the act.

His lips brush mine. He pulls away. Calls me Lov-lay and then does it again.

I think, *I like the taste of his mouth.*

Tangy. Metallic. It sets the blood in my veins on fire and I lick inside his mouth to get more. He gives me a funny look, but then he keeises me again and I forget about the taste.

"Don't go down Below."

Mama is back. Standing over me in our cave. I wake, bleary, feeling the crack of dried mud flake off my feet. For a second my heart seizes, but then I'm up, almost as tall as her, taller when I straighten my back. I see the gray in her head and the stoop to her proud back and I bare my teeth at her. Who she to tell me no?

I rage. Who she to take my boy from me?

She flinch, eh! Flinch so hard, I think I hit her instead but no. We still. Just separate. Like Below and High.

We stare at each other until her hand snakes out, but she slow now, too slow. I'm fast. I take the hand and yank her forward, push her into the cave until it me that stand over her, sprawled out on the rock.

She make a sound when she land. Like rock on rock. For a second she flickers, smoke surrounds her, but when I blink, it clears like it was never there.

Orange licks across her dark eyes before they settle back to black.

"Please," she beg. I never hear her beg before. But it's not enough. Below inside me now. I want my boy. "Don't go down Below."

I snarl, turn around, and race down the steps until Below fills my nose and ears and eyes and threads through my toes. I look up. She's standing on our ledge, staring down.

"Nothing good come from Below," she whispers. I hear her as clear as if she say straight in my ear. "If you go, you never come back."

I know what she say. What she mean. But my gum burns, my stomach clenches. I turn and rush to *my* boy.

He'll find me, I think as I search and call for him. Like he always does. *Like he always will*, something whispers. All my veins will settle and my stomach will calm and my gums will stop throbbing as soon as he finds me and keeises me. When there's no Mama or mountain or Below or High. Just E-li-as and Lov-lay.

But he not there. He nowhere. I search and search until I get close to his town. I hide behind a border-tree, lay my hand against its trunk.

No heartbeat.

All the people, all the dead trees. This tree soul gone far inside and for the first time I feel annoyed. A heat rises, peaks at my head, makes it hot and my gums flare and then I hear a cry—like the thing that wails but closer. Softer. Smaller.

Something tells me stay away, and it sounds like Mama's voice, but I ignore it like I ignore her before and creep close to their village until my nose crinkles at the stench of them.

The cry comes again and I finally see why Mama said nothing good comes from Below.

They have ones like me. Dark like me. Pretty like me. But they're chained to walls to rocks, to men. They like me but not. Dead behind their eyes, their hearts beat fast, weak. One, a woman—I think for a second it's Mama, but her face too gaunt, her limbs bent weird, like they break and set and break and set.

She bare, apart from the chain around her waist, and each time a man who look like my boy hits her, her mouth opens with a wail. No one else is angry. All the other people just walk about, and laugh and sing while the man beats the one-of-me until her skin breaks and a spray of red lands across the ground and she crumple.

Anger comes quick, fills all my veins with burning, makes my skin itch inside, and I want to leap at the man—I want to break the hand that hits her. I almost do, too. But someone snatches my wrist and drags me away. I claw at their face, but they duck, push me into the tree, and then I see him, my boy. E-li-as.

My heart swells. He'll know what to do. My boy. E-li-as and Lov-lay.

I try to tell him what I saw—I try to make him feel the way I do—the anger inside, the fire in my face and the itch, like ants across my bones, beneath my skin. But he's frowning, shaking his head. Cupping my face between his rough, pale hands.

"All right," he says. But it's not all right and I make to push him away but he hold fast. "All right, Lov-lay. All right. Not—you. All right. Not—*you*."

I don't like the way he say *you*. Like I different. Like I didn't just see one-of-me-like-me beat until she fall.

"Him hit her like she a beast—but she one of me. One of you. Don't you see?" I cry.

But *my* boy doesn't see. He can't see. Can't hear, either. He never tried to mimic my words and so he doesn't understand and I see again, why Mama so afraid of Below.

"*You*—good ones. *You*—good." He swoops, keeises me again, but my lips are stiff. "*You*—good," he murmurs against my lips. "Not *them*, Lov-lay. Not yo—"

I push him. I hear the thud of his body against the ground, but I only look at him once before running.

I feel sick. Mama was right, eh? I shouldn't have left High. Nothing good comes from Below.

"Mama?" I call, but the forest strange—I can't find my way and then I hear another wail, this one old and deep, it shakes my bones within my skin and rattles every teeth. Each way I twist, the screaming grows louder until I press my hands against my ears to make it stop. But the sound in my head, oui? Inside my ears, inside my head and veins. My skin ripples, roiling over my skeleton, and then it stops and I look up and I see the Beast that wails and remember what I forgot all that time ago.

"Mama?" I call, to the bones tied to the tree.

Ain't no time for ones like we.

We born, then we die. But it too long between the two to keep count. Not many of us, but there are enough. All like me and Mama. Tall, thin, strong, and dark. We live up High in the mountain, all together. All as one.

They liked to watch too, just like me. And we'd watch for days and weeks and months and years. And when we were hungry, we would eat.

When I remember the tangy, metallic taste of food, I don't

know how I ever forgot it. And now I can't know how I've gone so long without it.

Long time passed, me and of-me watched and smiled and laughed and ate and one day the sea gave its first gift. Another wrecked ship. The *first* ship. The first gaggle of *others*.

Me and of-me tried to be kind—we tried to help. But they couldn't listen, rotten in their core, and they cut the trees and spoiled the streams with filth and black blood until the land began to die.

Mama and the others went to fight. We strong, eh? We strong like rock. But they too many and too greedy and bad and when they realized where we hide we skin, they trapped them all, naked and shivering from moonlight to first light and smiled while they all burned.

I watched, I too young. My skin didn't move like theirs yet, so they never found it to trap me. But I remember Mama—her eyes were good, eh? She find me in the shadows and she tell me one last thing as her skin burned and crackled and burst pus onto the ground.

"Stay High. Stay safe. Nothing good Below."

She not much now. Not even really bones. Storm take their color, time take their strength so they not much more than crumbling needles. But it she, eh? It she. I don't know where her sisters are—I don't know where the first settlers burned them. But the Beast—the thing that wails—the bones of my mama is quiet, oui? I finally see what I supposed to see, remember what I supposed to remember. So now she quiet. Now she rest.

My skin moves. I bring my hand to my face as the brown skin jumps and leaps and wiggles. It ready, eh? It ready to go. It ready to let me out.

My gums burn as new teeth descend and I smell with a new nose.

I go back. Find my boy by my sparkling. He's frowning, pacing. He turns, sees me in the shadows.

"Lov-lay," he calls. "Come."

And I do. His eyes not good, though. They not strong like mine. He doesn't *see* me until I'm at his throat, sniffing the vein that throbs, and his hands are sliding across my muscles and veins, getting tangled between sinew and coating in blood and he cries out, afraid, and something inside me clenches, happy. I push him back as he tries to get away. I push and push until we're in the water and then I look into his eyes and smile.

"Nothing good Below," I say, and then I do what my body has been begging me for all this time: I eat.

When I'm done, I push him down, down into the deepest parts of the water. Down where I used to wonder where my body would go if I could dip under the surface. I'm almost tempted, belly fat with life and content, to finally swim under, to see how far my sparkle goes. But my skin out there, and I think of the one-like-me in the camp. See the spurt of her infected blood after her skin breaks and I know I can eat more tonight.

About the Authors

Erica Waters (she/her) grew up in the pine woods of rural Florida, though she now resides in Nashville, Tennessee. She has a Master's degree in English and works as a university writing tutor. She is the author of *Ghost Wood Song* and *The River Has Teeth*.

Chloe Gong (she/her) is the *New York Times* bestselling author of *These Violent Delights* and its sequel, *Our Violent Ends*, as well as *Foul Lady Fortune*. She is a recent graduate of the University of Pennsylvania, where she double majored in English and international relations. Born in Shanghai and raised in Auckland, New Zealand, Chloe is now located in New York pretending to be a real adult.

Tori Bovalino (she/her) is originally from Pittsburgh, Pennsylvania, and now lives in the UK with her partner and their very loud cat, Sir Gordon Greenidge II. Tori loves scary stories, obscure academic book facts, and impractical oversized sweaters.

Hannah Whitten (she/her) has been writing to amuse herself since she could hold a pen, and sometime in high school, figured out that what amused her might also amuse others. When she's not writing, she's reading, making music, or attempting to bake. She lives in an old farmhouse in Tennessee with her husband, children, too many pets, and probably some ghosts. Her debut novel, *For the Wolf*, was an instant *New York Times* and *USA Today* bestseller, and the sequel, *For the Throne*, released in summer 2022.

Allison Saft (she/her) is the author of eerie and critically acclaimed romantic fantasies, *Down Comes the Night* and *A Far Wilder Magic*. After receiving her MA in English literature from Tulane University, she moved from the Gulf Coast to the West Coast, where she spends her time hiking the redwoods and practicing aerial silks.

Olivia Chadha (she/her) is the author of the YA sci-fi duology *Rise of the Red Hand* and *Fall of the Iron Gods*, and the adult novel *Balance of Fragile Things*. She can be found at www.oliviachadha.com.

Courtney Gould (she/her) writes books about queer girls, ghosts, and things that go bump in the night. Her debut novel, *The Dead and the Dark* released August 2021. She graduated from Pacific Lutheran University in 2016 with a Bachelor's degree in creative writing and publishing. She was born and raised in Salem, Oregon, where she continues to write speculative, queer mysteries about lonely places and lonely girls.

Aden Polydoros (he/him) is an author of YA dark fantasy and gothic horror novels, and has a bachelor's degree in English from Northern Arizona University. His most recent novel, *The City Beautiful*, was declared a Best YA Book of 2021 by New York Public Library, BookPage, Buzzfeed, and Tor.com and was the winner of the 2022 Sydney Taylor Book Award for Young Adult Fiction. His gothic fantasy novel, *Bone Weaver*, comes out in September 2022 from Inkyard Press/HarperCollins.

Alex Brown (she/her) is a YA horror writer who loves rooting for the final girl—especially if she's also a monster. Alex is a queer, biracial Filipino American, and one of the co-creators of *The Bridge*, a haunted, folklore-filled audio drama podcast that has over 1,000,000 downloads to date! When she's not writing, she works in the entertainment industry, most recently serving as the showrunner's assistant on *Supernatural* and the *Resident Evil* and *Grendel* adaptations for Netflix. As far as she knows, she hasn't left anyone behind in a creepy tunnel. But that could always change.

Shakira Toussaint (she/her) grew up in West London, dreaming of fantasy worlds and islands drifting in the blue. She holds a BA in film and English and an MA in creative writing. She writes about monstrous women, mythology, and the Caribbean and can usually be found loudly complaining about the meat-to-gravy ratio in her curry goat.